T0322934

DEDICATED TO

Katie, Anna
and Jane Simms

Published in the UK by Scholastic, 2021
Euston House, 24 Eversholt Street, London, NW1 1DB
Scholastic Ireland, 89E Lagan Road, Dublin Industrial Estate,
Glasnevin, Dublin, D11 HP5F

Text © Rachel Pierce, 2022

Cover illustration, endpaper and border illustrations by Jennifer Davison

Illustrations by Donough O'Malley, Erin Brown, Eva Byrne,
Linda Fahrlin, Lydia Hughes, Róisín Hahessy & Úna Woods

The extract from Thomas McGlue's testimony on pages 84–85
is used with the permission of the Guinness Archive.

ISBN 978 07023 1854 2

A CIP catalogue record for this book is available from the British Library.

Printed in the UK by Bell and Bain Ltd, Glasgow
Paper made from wood grown in sustainable forests and
other controlled sources.

1 3 5 7 9 10 8 6 4 2

www.scholastic.co.uk

Any website addresses listed in the book are correct at the
time of going to print. However, please be aware that online content
is subject to change and websites can contain or offer content that
is unsuitable for children. We advise all children be
supervised when using the internet.

WRITTEN BY RACHEL PIERCE

BEDTIME STORIES

INCREDIBLE Irish Tales FROM THE PAST

ILLUSTRATED BY
DONOUGH O'MALLEY, ERIN BROWN,
EVA BYRNE, JENNIFER DAVISON,
LINDA FAHRLIN, LYDIA HUGHES,
RÓISÍN HAHESSY & ÚNA WOODS

SCHOLASTIC

CONTENTS

THE STORY OF
A STOLEN HEART

IMAGINE BEING THE SON OF A KING, BORN INTO A HAPPY LIFE, AND THEN BECOMING A CHILD-HOSTAGE, MISTREATED FROM DAWN UNTIL DUSK. THIS WAS HOW LORCÁN Ó TUATHAIL (LAURENCE O'TOOLE) STARTED OUT IN LIFE. SO HOW DID HIS HEART END UP THE SUBJECT OF A DARING THEFT? AND WHY WOULD ANYONE WANT TO STEAL A DEAD MAN'S HEART? WELL, THAT'S A LONG STORY…

We have to go all the way back to 1128, hundreds of years ago – that's when Laurence was born in Castledermot, County Kildare. His father, Muirchertach, was the king of northern Leinster. In those times, it could be as dangerous to be wealthy as it was to be poor – and young Laurence learned that the hard way. When he was ten years old, his father sent him as a hostage to Dermot MacMurrough, king of Leinster, as a sign that there would be peace between the two kings. The young boy was like a living contract, guaranteeing that his father wouldn't cause any trouble for MacMurrough.

It would have been easy to treat the young boy well and see he came to no harm, but that doesn't seem to have been MacMurrough's way. Instead, he clapped young Laurence in chains and sent him to a remote part of the country, away from everything and everyone Laurence knew. He barely fed or clothed him and let the weather wreak its worst on him. It must have been a terrible ordeal for such a young boy, especially as he

15

would have been used to a very nice life with his high-born family. What manner of loneliness would you feel if you were spirited away on your own and treated as if you'd committed some terrible crime?

Laurence endured this life for two years, but eventually his father managed to arrange for his son to be sent to stay with the community of monks at Glendalough in County Wicklow. There, things were much better for Laurence – he was taken care of and educated, and he became devoted to the monks' way of life. His father agreed he could stay on and live there, which he gladly did. In 1153 Laurence was made abbot of the monastery, even though he was only twenty-five years old. His fellow monks considered him to be kind and wise and intelligent. He had found his true calling.

Glendalough is a beautiful and peaceful place. There are hills and lakes and a great sense of stillness – the perfect place to quietly worship God. But medieval Ireland wasn't a very peaceful country. Laurence couldn't sit in his lovely Glendalough and do nothing. He was appointed archbishop of Dublin in 1162 and he moved to the city – a far cry from his peaceful monastery. He took up residence at Christ Church Cathedral, which became dear to his heart.

In 1169 it was all change again when the Normans arrived from England, under the leadership of the fearsome Richard de Clare, also known as Richard fitz Gilbert, and who people called Strongbow (which is a lot of names for one man!). There was war and hardship. Laurence worked hard to negotiate with the Normans, trying to keep the fragile peace. He was devastated to see so many of the citizens being killed by the newcomers, and he did all he could to protect and house them. He was forever looking for ways to help the poor and tried in vain to make peace between Ireland and England. This was a devilishly hard task that he would struggle with until the end of his days.

He left Ireland in 1180, on a peace mission to try to get King Henry II of England onside. The king wasn't interested in a holy man's opinion on the matter, however. Lorcan followed the king to France, still trying to persuade him, still failing. Finally, Laurence fell ill in Normandy, France, and a community of monks there cared for him until his death on 14 November 1180. And there he was buried, in the crypt beneath the monastery, never to see Ireland again.

But now there's a twist to the story – because some of Laurence did see Ireland again. The Catholic Church has a long history of preserving and venerating to sacred relics – holy objects associated with a saint. After his death, Laurence was put on the road to sainthood because of his dedication to God and his life of 'heroic virtue'. He was finally canonized (meaning he was declared a saint) in 1225 and became St Laurence O'Toole. This was cause for celebration in Ireland as St Laurence O'Toole became the patron saint of Dublin, and also cause for gathering sacred relics of this newly sainted man. His heart and some bones were collected from his tomb and his heart was brought back to Ireland, to Christ Church Cathedral.

As was the custom, Laurence's heart was placed into a reliquary. This is a specially built 'house' for a sacred relic. A wooden heart-shaped box was made to hold the precious heart, the box was placed inside a square iron cage, and it was put on display, where the faithful would pray to Laurence to heal them or to help them. And there Laurence's heart stayed, for centuries, until one night in 2012.

It sounds like a scary idea to steal a sacred relic. Really, you'd be expecting some sort of divine revenge. It's audacious, to say the least. But someone decided to do just that.

On 3 March 2012, that someone went to visit Christ Church Cathedral, like all the other visitors milling around inside the beautiful cathedral. But as the light faded and the doors were locked for the night, this person hid somewhere in that huge building – and no one noticed them. After the steps of the caretaker had echoed into the distance and the last door had slammed shut, that someone would have been totally alone in the darkness of the cathedral, with all the statues' eyes watching them. It must have been eerie. It must have been cold. But then perhaps they didn't notice because they had work to do.

They came out of their hiding place and stole over to the reliquary in the Chapel of St Laud, ignoring the gold candlesticks and gold chalices that would have been of huge interest to a greedy thief. No, they had only one object in their sights. A metal-cutting tool snipped and prised at the bars of the cage, until finally the box was freed. They reached in and carefully removed the heart. For the first time since the thirteenth century, St Laurence O'Toole's heart was not in its resting place. Perhaps the thief stood there, uncertain, wondering whether this really was a good idea – but they still took the heart. Then they went over to the Trinity altar and lit two candles. Was that to say sorry to the saint?

Once the doors opened for visitors the next morning, the thief mingled with the crowd and left – taking the sacred relic with them.

For six years, no one knew who had taken the relic or what they had done with it. The Gardaí (the Irish police) searched and questioned, but there were no clues. They checked the CCTV footage of the people entering and leaving the cathedral that morning, but no heart-napping thief was spotted. It was a dead end, a perfect crime. The whole of Dublin was distraught at the loss of such a precious relic, but no one had any idea where to begin looking for it. The heart of St Laurence O'Toole was gone.

And then – another twist in the story! Newspaper reports in 2018 told how someone called the Gardaí and made a confession: they had taken the heart, but now they desperately wanted to give it back because they believed it had cursed them. They said, 'It only brought bad luck.' A number of their family members had died of heart attacks. Heart attacks. They believed the saint was making a point. So they told the Gardaí where the sacred relic could be found: in the Phoenix Park in Dublin. And it was there, just where the sorry thief had said it would be.

As you can imagine, everyone at Christ Church Cathedral was overjoyed when they received the news. The relic was completely undamaged – they didn't have a broken heart on their hands, thankfully. The Gardaí brought the sacred relic back and, at long last, it could be rehoused in the safety of the saint's beloved Christ Church Cathedral.

To this day, no one has been arrested for stealing the heart of St Laurence. But if those newspaper reports are true and someone did make that phone call and did talk about a curse, then it would seem the thief has already received a heart-breaking punishment for stealing the heart away.

. . . .

EXPLORE THE STORY

You can visit **Christ Church Cathedral** in Dublin to see the returned sacred relic of St Laurence O'Toole. His feast day is 14 November, if you want to go on a special day.

You can also visit the remains of the monastic community at **Glendalough**, in County Wicklow, to see where St Laurence O'Toole's story started. It's very beautiful there – and be sure to bring your walking boots so you can enjoy all the beautiful walks around this peaceful place.

. . . .

ILLUSTRATED BY EVA BYRNE

THE STORY OF A FORMIDABLE COUNTESS

IF YOU WERE BORN A WOMAN IN TWELFTH-CENTURY IRELAND, WHAT WOULD YOUR LIFE HAVE BEEN LIKE? IF YOU WERE POOR, IT WOULD HAVE BEEN VERY TOUGH. YOUR HOUSE WAS COLD, YOUR CLOTHES WERE THIN AND YOUR CHILDREN WERE ALWAYS LOOKING AT YOU WITH HUNGER. POOR PEOPLE USUALLY LIVED HARD AND DIED YOUNG. IF YOU WERE WEALTHY, YOU HAD FINE CLOTHES AND BIG FIREPLACES AND GOOD FOOD TO EAT, BUT YOU WERE STILL ONLY A WOMAN, SO NO ONE REALLY CARED WHAT YOU THOUGHT ABOUT ANYTHING – INCLUDING WHO YOUR HUSBAND SHOULD BE! BUT WHAT IF YOU WERE THE KIND OF WOMAN WHO DIDN'T WANT TO BE QUIET AND OBEDIENT – WHAT THEN?

Isabel de Clare was the daughter of a strong woman, and both of their marriages changed the course of Irish history, which is a pretty incredible claim for any wedding!

Isabel's mother was Aoife, daughter of the king of Leinster, Dermot MacMurrough. He was forever battling to retain his lands and power. He invited Anglo-Norman lords from Wales to come and fight on his behalf, with the blessing of King Henry II. Among these lords was Strongbow (Richard de Clare). He was a mighty soldier, and he came over to Ireland in 1170 with the promise that if he fought for Dermot, he could marry Dermot's daughter. Strongbow did help Dermot regain his kingdom, and in that same year he collected his prize: the hand of Aoife in marriage. This meant that when Dermot died, the kingship of Leinster would pass to Strongbow through his wife, so he was getting a very good deal all round. Luckily for Strongbow, Dermot died in 1171, so he didn't have long to wait for the really big prize!

Aoife and Strongbow had two children, Isabel and Gilbert. They were born into a world of great privilege, at a time when the king of England was in charge of Ireland too. Their father died in 1176, when they were both very young. Just under ten years later, in 1185, Gilbert died, leaving Isabel as the sole heir to her parents' vast wealth. She had to live at the royal court in London until she came of age, when the king of England would choose a husband for her – and she would have no say whatsoever in the matter.

Isabel's marriage was of utmost importance because she was now the richest heiress anyone had ever heard of at the time. Through her parents, she owned lands in Ireland, England, Wales and France, and, thanks to the laws of the time, she would inherit everything through her mother. So her husband had to be chosen carefully, to ensure all those lands and titles and money remained loyal to the king of England.

Isabel stayed under the watchful eyes of the royal household while she grew up and became a teenager. Perhaps this was all very normal for Isabel, but it sounds strange to us – to lose your father and your mother and your brother and then have to wait around to be married off. But no one ever asked Isabel what she thought or felt about it, so we'll never know. But whatever she might have felt, it didn't matter. In 1189, when she was about seventeen, she was told her husband had been chosen – and that her first time to meet him would be on her wedding day.

King Henry had chosen carefully, and he had chosen William Marshal, one of the greatest knights the world had ever seen. He was much older than Isabel, about forty when they married, but he was extremely brave on behalf of the

Crown and extremely loyal, and Isabel was his reward. It was some reward! When Isabel became his wife, William suddenly inherited vast lands in Ireland, Britain and Europe – and the lordship of Leinster.

Even though their marriage was arranged like a chess move – it was all about strategy and nothing to do with love – it seems that Isabel and William really did fall for each other. She supported him in all things. They had ten children – five boys and five girls. And Isabel travelled with William and did everything in her power to help him keep hold of her inheritance – which was no easy matter in the warring medieval period.

In the 1200s, Isabel and William founded many towns and buildings together, including Tintern Abbey and New Ross in County Wexford. They also restored the town of Kilkenny and its castle, which became their main base in Leinster. Of course, when you have lots of wealth and property, people are anxious to

take it from you – and this was certainly the case in Ireland. Things were getting very difficult in 1207, when war broke out yet again in Leinster. At the same time, William was in trouble with the king of England, and eventually the king demanded William return to London. Isabel was pregnant, but she insisted that she would mind things in Ireland while he was gone. That took some courage but fighting for their lands was just as important to her as it was to her husband. William asked the lords of Leinster to protect their lady, then he left. If he was betting that his wife could look after herself, he was right.

Isabel was in Kilkenny Castle when William's main rival in Leinster, Meilyr fitz Henry, came looking for a fight. He set up a siege of the castle, no doubt banking on Isabel – a mere woman – caving in. The last thing Isabel was going to do was hand over her castle. She didn't have many men with her, so that was the first problem to solve. One unlucky soldier was chosen to be lowered on a rope all the way down from the battlements, so he could run and tell her supporters about what was happening. When the local people heard the news, they rushed to the castle to help her, defeated fitz Henry and his men, and saved the castle – just as Isabel had planned.

Once she had Meilyr fitz Henry where she wanted him, Isabel demanded he submit to her and that he hand over his son as a guarantee that he wouldn't set upon them again. She forced other rebel knights to hand over their sons as well, to ensure cooperation. This would have been a huge humiliation for fitz Henry – to be outsmarted and defeated by a pregnant woman. We can only imagine the look on William's face when he received the news in London!

William fell ill in January 1219, and it was clear death was not far off. His family gathered around him. It is said that he asked Isabel and his five daughters to sing for him and they did so, singing their husband and father towards death. In the final hours, William chose to take the vows to become a knight Templar, but doing so meant Isabel would not be able to physically touch him afterwards because Templars were not permitted to kiss any woman. It is recorded that William said to Isabel, **'Fair lady, kiss me now, for you will never be able to do so again.'** She stepped forward and kissed him, and both of them wept.

William was buried in Temple Church in London, but his wife did not join him there. Isabel was buried in Tintern Abbey in Wales, beside her mother, Aoife. Those two strong women are joined forever in death. There is a story you'll hear told in New Ross, about a slab in the graveyard at St Mary's Church that bears the inscription 'Isabel Laegn', which has been translated as Isabel Leinster. Some believe it marks the spot where Isabel's heart was buried. While her body lies in Wales, it is suggested that her heart was returned to Ireland, to remain there. This has never been proved, but somehow it seems right and fitting that Isabel de Clare would have left her heart in Ireland.

EXPLORE THE STORY

You can see the spectacular painting of *The Marriage of Strongbow and Aoife*, by Daniel Maclise, in the National Gallery of Ireland.

In the Exhibition Centre in New Ross, you can see the unique **Ros Tapestry**, which depicts the marriages of Aoife and of Isabel.

ILLUSTRATED BY ÚNA WOODS

THE STORY OF A KIDNAPPED VILLAGE

YOU HAVE NO DOUBT HEARD TALES OF PIRATES – ABOUT THE FEAR THAT GRIPPED THE HEARTS OF THOSE WHO SAW A MENACING SHIP ON THE HORIZON. THAT'S THE THING ABOUT FIRESIDE TALES, THEY PLANT IMAGES IN OUR MINDS THAT CLING TIGHT, CONJURING UP VIVID, FEVERISH DREAMS FOR US WHEN WE CLOSE OUR EYES. WE TELL OURSELVES NOT TO BE SILLY – IT'S AN OLD STORY, A LEGEND OR A MADE-UP BOGEYMAN. BUT EVERY NOW AND THEN, A FEAR CAN TAKE SHAPE AND SOME POOR SOUL FINDS THEMSELVES IN A WAKING NIGHTMARE. THAT'S WHAT HAPPENED TO THE VILLAGERS OF BALTIMORE…

It is said that the darkest hour is before dawn, and it was in this dark hour that the ships slid into Baltimore harbour, off west Cork, on 20 June 1631. The oar blades were treated with a special substance to ensure that they made no sound in the water, no splash or slap that would give the game away. These were seasoned pirates who knew all the tricks of their trade. On this night, for what is recorded as the very first and the very last time, they had set their sights on Ireland. The sleeping and snoring villagers had no earthly clue what was about to happen.

The men who left their small boats and crept quietly ashore were Barbary corsairs from North Africa. They were under the command of Morat Rais, born as Jan Jansen, also known as Captain John. Rais was a Dutchman who was taken as a slave when he was working on the island of Lanzarote. He went on to become a feared pirate raider, stealing people from all over the world and turning them into slaves. One thing was for sure: when the pirate fleet of Morat Rais turned up in your harbour, you knew you were in serious trouble.

On this night, the village of Baltimore was about to find out why these pirates were so feared. This sort of attack had never been seen before on the island, and people still argue to this day about what made them come so far and what made them choose Baltimore. Did some local person have a devious plan, a hidden motive? Whatever the reason, they came determined to capture some valuable slaves for the North African market.

Alongside the fearsome corsairs were the even more fearsome janissaries. They were part of an elite fighting force and wore red waistcoats and plumes in their caps. As well as guns, they carried sabres, curved and deadly. The corsairs were armed with muskets and iron bars, to prise open shut doors and get at the inhabitants cowering inside. About 230 of these armed and dangerous men swarmed onto the shore at Baltimore, and all the while the villagers slept soundly, hearing nothing.

Down near the harbour was the Cove, where the thatched cottages of the fishing folk huddled together, about twenty-six in all. Morat Rais planned to start here. His men split up into twenty-six groups, each standing in front of one cottage. Still moving with the quietness of mice, they raised firebrands and set fire to the thatch. The cottages quickly started to burn. Shocked awake and stupefied with sleepiness, the people inside dashed from their beds and raced to get outside. Imagine their utter confusion when they were confronted by these bands of pirates. They must have pinched themselves – but it was no dream.

The pirates rounded up about a hundred people, including pregnant women and the elderly. They quickly marched them down to the waiting boats and

spirited them away to the waiting ships, silhouetted on the edge of the shadowy darkness. Once they were safely stowed way, Morat Rais led his men back along the road, this time towards the main village.

In the village, people were curled up in their warm beds, savouring the last hours of sleep before the sun rose. But one man was restless – something was tugging at his tired mind. William Harris got up to investigate and looked out the window, towards the Cove. He saw the flames, the men moving about, and his blood ran cold in his veins. Attackers!

Whatever was happening out there, William was the only one who had any chance of raising the alarm. He readied his musket gun. There was very little time. They were coming. His neighbours were nowhere in sight – they must all be lost to sleep in the dead of night. Whatever tiny chance there was for them

to escape, it lay in William's hands. He went outside, raised his gun and shot a silence-shattering blast into the night sky, towards the stars.

Soon after, the well-organized attackers once again went house to house in the village, using their iron bars to crack open doors. But where were all the people? The houses seemed empty. They found only about ten people, even though they burst open about thirty doors. They had expected at least a hundred more valuable slaves – what had happened?

Up above them, musket fire rang out. They would have known there were regiments of English soldiers about, but the nearest was miles away. So who was firing off gunshots? The sound of the gun was joined by another sound – a drum beating out a war call. William's neighbour had heard his warning shot and leaped into action, banging his drum as loud as he could – sounding like a regiment in full march. But it was just two men, desperately trying to ward off a fate worse than death. It was just a clever deception – but could it work?

Morat Rais was an old hand at this raiding business, and he knew the crucial thing was to grab what you could and get away safely. Faced with this unexpected resistance, he did just that – he told his men to take the ten people they'd found and all make their way back to the boats and onto the ships. Their night's work was done. They had stolen away almost a village-full of people – about 107 in all, fifty of those children – and these slaves would translate into a good payday when they brought them to the slave market of Algiers.

The journey across the oceans must have been hellish for the villagers, and their arrival at Algiers would have been even worse. They were separated from each other and paraded about for potential owners to stare at them and place bids. They would have been judged on their strength and their beauty and their skills. The lives they had known were far, far away and they were in a land

34

that would have been very strange to them, under a blazing hot sun, all rights and liberties stripped from them along with their Irish clothes. They must have thought they would never again see home.

The truth is, very few of them ever did. For fifteen long years, they lived as slaves – some on the galley ships, some in households, some on farms. They had probably long given up hope when Edmund Cason arrived on his ship, the *Charles*, carrying money to pay ransoms for the English and Irish men and women who had been captured. The slave owners agreed to accept money in exchange for their slaves, but the prices kept going higher and higher. In the end, of around 650 listed slaves, Cason had to accept he could only afford to ransom about 240. Among the names of those lucky 240 people were just two from Baltimore – Joane Broadbrook and Ellen Hawkins. Everyone else had died, or disappeared, or no longer wanted to travel back to Ireland. So it was just these two women who would return to tell the tale of what happened on the night the village disappeared.

....

EXPLORE THE STORY
The **Baltimore Pirate Festival** commemorates the Sack of Baltimore and takes place annually on 16 to 18 June.

....

ILLUSTRATED BY ERIN BROWN

THE STORY OF A RECKLESS SCOUNDREL

DID YOU KNOW THAT STEALING THE CROWN JEWELS FROM THE TOWER OF LONDON COUNTS AS HIGH TREASON? IN THE 1600S, THE PUNISHMENT FOR THIS CRIME WAS TO BE HUNG, DRAWN AND QUARTERED. THIS WAS A REALLY GRUESOME DEATH THAT INVOLVED BEING TIED TO A PANEL AND DRAGGED ALONG THE GROUND BY A HORSE, WHICH RACED YOU TO YOUR PLACE OF EXECUTION. THERE, YOU WERE HUNG BY THE NECK UNTIL JUST ABOUT DEAD AND THEN, FINALLY, YOU WERE BEHEADED, DISEMBOWELLED AND SLICED INTO FOUR QUARTERS. AFTER ALL THAT, THE VARIOUS BITS OF YOU MIGHT BE SENT AROUND THE COUNTRY AS A WARNING TO ANY OTHER WOULD-BE TRAITORS. EVEN THINKING ABOUT IT IS ENOUGH TO MAKE YOU FEEL FAINT! SO, WOULD YOU HAVE RISKED IT BY TRYING TO STEAL THE JEWELS? NOT LIKELY! BUT COLONEL THOMAS BLOOD THOUGHT DIFFERENTLY.

If Captain Jack Sparrow ever went truly rogue, he would become like Colonel Thomas Blood, a man who looked after his own interests in all things and by any means – including masterful disguises. He led a long and extremely colourful life, careening from one adventure to the next, and often from one dangerously bad idea to the next. His was a fearless life of daring and rebellion and hair's-breadth escapes. On top of all this, there is an unsolved mystery at the heart of his story.

Thomas Blood is thought to have been born in County Clare around 1618, although he also spent time in Sarney, County Meath. He lived mainly in

England and married an Englishwoman. He was there for the Civil War in 1642 and he chose to fight on the side of the Crown, but when he realized that Oliver Cromwell was going to defeat the king's forces, he switched sides. Who knows where his loyalty truly lay – perhaps only with his own fortune. Cromwell rewarded him with lands in Ireland, and all was well until 1660. That year, the Crown was restored and King Charles II took the throne – putting Blood on the wrong side again. He left for Ireland with his family to escape any revenge the king might have in mind.

Running away didn't work because the king made sure Blood's lands in Ireland were taken away from him. Now it was Blood's turn to think about revenge. He decided on a dangerous plan to attack the English rulers, who were, after all, the king's men in Ireland. Everyone from Dublin to London was shocked when Blood and a group of men tried to storm Dublin Castle and take prisoner the lord lieutenant of Ireland, James Butler, Duke of Ormonde. They failed, and Blood escaped to Europe and kept his head low for a while. But then, cheeky as ever, he nipped back across into England using a different name and setting himself up as a doctor. Maybe the disguises didn't have to be quite so masterful back then!

Blood hadn't forgotten about the duke and his nearly successful kidnap, and he decided to have another go at him – this time to kill him. He gathered some men, watched the duke to find out his daily movements, then lay in wait for him on a street in Piccadilly, London. The element of surprise worked in their favour, and Blood and his men managed to bundle up the duke and carry him off. Their plan was to hang him at Tyburn, the main place for execution in London – and they very nearly did. But the duke managed to escape at the last moment.

You might think Colonel Blood would trade in his madcap plans for a quiet life now, but you'd be very wrong. He began to plot out the most daring and most dangerous adventure of his life: to steal the Crown Jewels. The jewels were kept – as they still are – under lock, key and guard in the Tower of London, and no one had ever tried to steal them before. In fact, no one has ever tried to steal them since. Colonel Blood is the only person who ever came close to committing such an extraordinary crime.

His well-laid plan had a few stages. The first step was to make friends with the keeper of the jewels. This was Talbot Edwards, a man of around eighty, who lived in private rooms in the Tower with his wife, so that he remained close to the priceless treasure at all times. This must have been great news for Blood, to find out that the guard was an elderly man. He wouldn't have to take on a king's army to gain his prize!

One day, a very nice parson visited the Tower, to view the jewels with his very lovely wife. They were shown around by Mr Edwards. By all accounts, the

parson's wife was suddenly taken ill, and the kindly keeper and his wife brought the couple to their room to allow her to rest. That was it: Blood – disguised as the parson – was in. He became a regular and welcome visitor, bringing gifts and charming the elderly couple. On one visit, he brought a wonderful suggestion: his handsome and wealthy young nephew should marry the Edwards' daughter. It was arranged that he would bring his nephew to visit.

When 'Parson' Blood turned up with three young men, all on horseback, Mr Edwards wasn't alarmed. When the men said they'd love to see the famous Crown Jewels, Mr Edwards wasn't alarmed. When they entered the strongroom together, Mr Edwards wasn't alarmed. But when his friend the parson suddenly knocked him to the ground, muffling and gagging him and whacking him with a mallet, Mr Edwards must have been very alarmed indeed.

The heist happened quickly. The men pulled away the metal grille protecting the treasure. St Edward's Crown was bulky and awkward, so Blood used another whack from his mallet to flatten it somewhat and then put it in a bag. The orb was a handy size, so one of Blood's men quickly stuffed it down his trousers to hide it. The sceptre was very long, and an attempt was made to cut it down to size. But the delay had given Mr Edwards time to come to his senses and he began roaring, 'Murder!' and 'Treason!' Time to flee the scene!

They ran, but Blood was captured by the guards, and all of the jewels were recovered. Surely, he was thinking of the fate that awaited him for committing high treason? No, he was still plotting a way out, telling everyone who asked that he would speak of the matter only to the king himself. And this is where the mystery lies: Charles II not only agreed to meet with Blood, but pardoned him – and gave him a pension of £500 per year and reinstated his lands in Ireland. People were agog at this. The pardon forgave the bold Blood everything.

Why on Earth would Charles II do this? Unfortunately, no one knows the truth of what the two men said to one another – what it was that convinced the king he needed Blood alive and onside. It's a mystery. It's thought that one of the conditions was that Blood worked for the Crown as a spy – work, you would imagine, that would suit the slippery Blood very well.

So, Colonel Thomas Blood lived to tell the tale – and lived very well under the king's favour, no doubt. His wild ways finally came to an end in 1680, when, at the age of 62, he died at his home in Bowling Abbey, Westminster. He wasn't laid to rest in Ireland, but was buried at the Church of St Margaret, Westminster.

There was, however, one final extraordinary chapter to his story. His life of deception and dark doings led to rumours that he had faked his death to escape a debt, that he was having the last laugh.

One week after his burial, his grave was dug up again and his body taken out – just to be absolutely sure he was dead. He was.

EXPLORE THE STORY
The **National Archives of the United Kingdom** hold documents relating to Colonel Blood, including the king's proclamation on the theft and Blood's pardon.

You can visit the never-stolen Crown Jewels at the **Tower of London**.

ILLUSTRATED BY LYDIA HUGHES

THE STORY OF A QUIET LIFE AND AN EXTRAORDINARY DEATH

A 'QUIET LIFE' DOESN'T NECESSARILY MEAN A NORMAL AND BORING LIFE. YOU CAN QUIETLY GO ABOUT DOING INCREDIBLE THINGS, BUT NOT SHOUTING ABOUT IT FROM THE ROOFTOPS. SOME PEOPLE ACHIEVE WONDERFUL THINGS AND YET NO ONE REALLY HEARS ABOUT IT UNTIL THEY ARE LONG DEAD. BUT WOULDN'T IT BE ODD TO LIVE A QUIET LIFE FILLED WITH WONDERFUL ACCOMPLISHMENTS, ONLY FOR YOUR DEATH TO BE SO UNIQUE THAT IT ENDED UP BEING THE MOST FAMOUS THING ABOUT YOU?

In the Victorian period, examining hidden worlds through microscopes became a very popular hobby for the rich. Early, simple microscopes had been in use since the 1500s, but they weren't used by scientists. People liked to build their own, figuring out the lenses and angles as they went along. This was how Anton van Leeuwenhoek did it. He is said to be the first person to view bacteria, using one of his own home-made microscopes. That must have been a really strange moment – to mount a specimen of his own saliva or blood on a needle under a lens and then to suddenly see that it was teeming with tiny, invisible life – a whole other world not seen by the naked eye. You can imagine how gazing through a lens could quickly become an obsession.

In the 1800s, microscopes were being made commercially and the lenses were getting better and better, so the magnification was getting bigger and bigger. The secret, minute details of insects and leaves could be seen and recorded. This was what first captured the imagination of Mary Ward (born Mary King in 1827). When she was just a little girl, she was fascinated by insects and butterflies and made collections of them. She then used her father's magnifying glass to examine her tiny captives.

Mary was very lucky that her family was wealthy and encouraged her passion. The sciences were certainly not seen as something that should be of interest to women. But Mary was hugely interested – so much so that her parents bought her a microscope of her own when she was a teenager. She spent all her time making her own slides from ivory, gathering specimens, looking carefully and then drawing and writing about what she saw.

In 1854 Mary married Henry Ward, and they spent time every year in his ancestral home in Ireland, Castle Ward in County Down. They had eight children, and Mary looked after them while Henry travelled and worked. But Mary didn't let that keep her from her passion. She spent every spare moment with her microscope and took it with her everywhere she went. Other ladies might have been packing combs and creams in their travel bags, but Mary made sure to have her microscope, slides and artist materials. She was constantly honing her skills as an artist, so she could make very detailed drawings of all that her microscope revealed to her.

She put her work together into a book called *Sketches with the Microscope* (1857). This showed just how good she had become – as a microscopist and as an artist. She was quite brilliant at her work. She wrote many more books, both for adults and children. She loved the idea of passing on her knowledge and encouraging children to be keen observers and artists.

While Mary was devoted to the smallnesses of our world and uncovering them, her cousin, William Parsons, the 3rd Earl of Rosse, was similarly passionate, but from quite a different perspective. Parsons lived in Birr Castle, County Offaly, and Mary was a frequent visitor there. You can just picture the two science-mad cousins walking the vast grounds, lost in fast-spilling conversation about all that science was revealing about the world. In the 1840s, William would have been talking about the giant telescope he was building – and no doubt Mary was just as excited about it as he was. In fact, on the grounds of Birr Castle, William ended up building the largest telescope in the world! He moved from the tiny worlds of the microscope to the wide world of the galaxies in the skies above. The telescope was called the 'Leviathan' because of its immense size, and Mary got to see it being built, bit by bit, making sketches of each stage in the process as she watched.

So, alongside her cousin, Mary moved between the once-invisible microscopic things of Earth to the once-invisible majestic monsters of space. She was equally fascinated by all of them, studying, observing, drawing her findings, and writing letters to some of the greatest scientific minds of her age, such as William Rowan Hamilton. She couldn't go to university, because she was a woman, wife and mother, but she used every means possible to reach out to other scientists, learn from them and share knowledge with them.

It must have been a truly wonderful moment when her dedication and contributions to the subject were recognized by the Royal Astronomical Society. The society took the step of putting Mary on its mailing list, which sounds like nothing much at all, but in fact she was one of only three women who had this honour bestowed on them, the other two being Queen Victoria and the Scottish scientist Mary Somerville.

Mary died very young, at only forty-two years of age. If she had lived longer, she no doubt would have achieved so much more and left many more books and artworks behind, but it wasn't to be. In 1869 she was visiting Birr Castle for a memorial service to mark the anniversary of William's death. In the true family spirit, another cousin, Charles Parsons, had designed and built a new invention: a steam-propelled carriage. You can imagine Mary marvelling at his ingenuity and being thrilled to experience this daring invention first-hand. She climbed in and they drove off. At a bend in the road, the carriage hit a pothole and Mary was flung out and onto the road, right under the steel wheels. Her neck was broken, and Mary died instantly. She is said to be the first person in Ireland to be killed in a car accident, and that's how she's often remembered, overshadowing the fact that her quiet life was filled with incredible achievements.

Although she died young, Mary left an important legacy, which is impressive for a woman of her time. There are her books and drawings, of course, which are still celebrated to this day, especially in County Offaly and at Castle Ward. And then there is the Leviathan itself. As the largest reflector telescope in the world, William's creation had drawn visitors from all over the world – it had a mirror 1.8 m (6 ft) wide and a tube 17.6 m (58 ft) long, very different from Mary's portable microscopes! He'd had to build walls 18 m (60 ft) high to support the telescope, and it stood on the lawn in front of the castle, an awe-inspiring sight. However, it was dismantled in 1914, and the giant mirror was donated to the Science Museum in London. Slowly, William's greatest achievement fell into disrepair.

It took decades before another Parsons had the vision to restore the Leviathan. In the 1980s, Brendan Parsons, the 7th Earl of Rosse, undertook this mammoth task, and the great telescope is now fully restored and open to the public. An important element in the restoration work was Mary Ward's work – her sketches of the building of the telescope were excellent source material when it was being brought back to life, along with photographs taken by William's wife, Mary Rosse.

When you record something of your own time, whether in writing or in drawing, you never can tell just how important it might prove to be one day. Mary might not have thought that her work would live so far beyond her, but her books and drawings and scientific insights will live on and on. It's like a gift she left for us. Given her love for teaching and sharing knowledge, it's safe to say that this would have delighted her.

EXPLORE THE STORY
You can visit the **Leviathan at Birr Castle**, County Offaly.

You can visit **Castle Ward**, County Down, where you can see Mary's equipment, writings and drawings all on display. This includes the actual microscope given to her by her parents when she was a teenager – the gift that was to lead to her life's work and legacy.

ILLUSTRATED BY RÓISÍN HAHESSY

THE STORY OF THE PLUCKY SS *SIRIUS*

I T WAS 4 APRIL 1838 AND THE WEATHER WAS FAIR. AT PASSAGE WEST HARBOUR, THE SMALL STEAMSHIP *SIRIUS* WAS PREPARING TO HEAD OUT INTO OPEN WATER, HER SIGHTS SET ON THE EAST COAST OF AMERICA. OVER IN BRISTOL HARBOUR, THE MIGHTY SS *GREAT WESTERN* WAS PREPARING FOR HER JOURNEY ACROSS THE ATLANTIC AS WELL. THEY WERE BOTH CHASING THE SAME PRIZE: THE FIRST STEAM-PROPELLED JOURNEY FROM EUROPE TO AMERICA. WHOEVER GOT THERE FIRST WOULD MAKE HISTORY. WHO WOULD WIN THE RACE – DAVID OR GOLIATH?

There is the romantic idea of sea travel and the harsh reality. In the eighteenth and nineteenth centuries, the reality was quite harsh indeed. People who bought tickets on sailing ships were taking their lives into their hands. If they weren't upended and drowned by battering waves and bad weather, they could easily catch infectious diseases in the cramped holds below deck where they had to wait out the crossing. And that waiting no doubt felt like an eternity. It took about three or four weeks to travel across the Atlantic to America, while ships coming the other way often took six weeks. Imagine being cooped up in a smelly, damp space with too many other people for weeks on end? And then add to that the chance of a pirate ship crossing your path and really ruining your trip. It was very far from cruise ships with on-board swimming pools and dining tables heaving with sumptuous food!

That's why people were so excited when the age of the steam ship was proclaimed. At last, there was a chance of crossing the ocean propelled by more than the wind and manpower. These ships were called paddle steamers. They had paddle wheels along the sides of the ship, like big water wheels. Water was heated in a boiler to produce steam, and the steam ran down pipes into a cylinder, pressuring a piston into motion, that in turn propelled the drive shaft into action, which caused the paddle wheels to turn. Steam ships had masts as a backup plan, but in theory they could travel entirely under their own ... well ... steam. This created a brand-new ambition for ship engineers: to build a steam ship that could complete a transatlantic crossing in record time.

One of the most famous ship engineers in the world undertook the challenge. Isambard Kingdom Brunel was a genius designer and engineer, and his very first steam ship was the SS *Great Western*. Brunel pictured sea travel as comfortable, swift and reliable, and he built his ships to deliver on this. He was a man who dreamed big – the *Great Western* was the largest steam ship ever built when it was completed: 72 m (236 ft) long, 17.6 m (58 ft) wide and able to carry 128 passengers and about sixty crew. While it was being built, the British and American Steam Navigation Company was busy building a rival ship, the SS *British Queen*. But disaster hit when the company collapsed and all work had to be halted. Brunel must have been pleased to hear that his major rival was land-bound, leaving the way open for his *Great Western* to clinch the title of first to travel the Atlantic.

But then disaster struck the *Great Western*. On 31 March 1838, as the ship sailed to Bristol, the starting point for the transatlantic run, the engine room reported a fire. As everyone rushed around trying to contain the fire, Brunel reportedly fell from a burning ladder and was injured. Poor Brunel had to go ashore and let the ship go on without him. And when news of the fire got out, lots of people cancelled their tickets and refused to join the historic trip. The whole enterprise was delayed, and it was only on 8 April that the *Great Western* could get underway – with only seven passengers to experience the journey.

It turned out that the *Great Western* was to have another rival, an unexpected one that joined the race late. The British and American Steam Navigation Company had accepted their chances were scuppered, but a businessman from Cork called James Beale suggested that they could charter a ship and have a go anyway. He suggested the SS *Sirius*, which must have seemed a silly idea given that it was much smaller, about 54 m (178 ft), and not built for long voyages. But Beale believed it could be done. He persuaded the company to back his plan and chose an experienced sailor, Lieutenant (Lt) Richard Roberts RN, to captain the *Sirius*.

The race was on.

The *Sirius* set off from Passage West, on Ireland's south coast, on 4 April with a crew of thirty-eight. Sirius is a star in the Canis Major constellation, otherwise known as the Dog Star. That's why her figurehead was a dog holding a star in its front paws. Crowds cheered them out of the harbour, then they were out into the wave-broken silence of the wide ocean. Lt Roberts was determined to use only steam power, even when the crew fought to raise the masts in bad weather. He prevailed. There is a story often told about the Sirius that they ran out of fuel and had to burn masts and furniture to complete the journey, but it wasn't true – just a delicious rumour! (Although Jules Verne added that scene to his book Around the World in Eighty Days.)

Finally, after just eighteen days, four hours and twenty-two minutes, the *Sirius* steamed into New York – it had arrived first, and the time of the crossing was sensational.

Crowds of people made their way to the port to see this historic ship arrive. The mayor of New York turned up to congratulate them, as well as top brass from the US army and navy, and Lt Roberts was greeted as a hero. He was granted the freedom of New York City, an honour given for very special achievements, and later the freedom of Cork and London as well. It was one huge party to celebrate a new age of travel between the continents.

The *Great Western* had left four days after the *Sirius*, but it nearly caught its rival – nearly, but not quite. Four hours after the exciting arrival of the *Sirius*, the *Great Western* steamed into view – to a rather muted welcome. Lt Hosken steered his great ship past the *Sirius*, and reports tell of the two ships 'exchanging salutes'. Well, you can picture the pinched, polite faces on one deck and the smirking faces on the other! It must have felt pretty good to Lt Roberts when this huge steamship had to take second place to his little ship.

Of course, the *Great Western* had made better time: it had left four days after the *Sirius* and nearly caught up with it. And when all the logbooks and records were examined, it turned out that it had sailed at an average of 8.66 knots (16 kmph), while the *Sirius* averaged 8.03 knots (14.9 kmph). Nonetheless the *Sirius* has gone down in history as the first steamship to cross the Atlantic.

The *Sirius* completed just one more transatlantic voyage, and then settled into what she was built for: the London–Cork route. The *Great Western* continued to cross the waters between Europe and America and the West Indies and enjoyed a long sailing life, before being scrapped in 1856.

The *Sirius* didn't enjoy such a good ending to its story. For her captain, after all the hoopla around his historic crossing, he went back to work, taking charge of the SS *President*. In March 1841 he left New York and headed back to Ireland, but the ship never arrived. It is presumed that it was wrecked in a storm mid-Atlantic, with all aboard lost forever. What exactly happened to them remains a mystery.

The *Sirius* itself fared no better. In January 1847, as the steamship made its way from Dublin to Cork, it met heavy fog near Ballycotton on the southeast coast. The ship hit a reef, though they managed to refloat it. But then it hit Smith's Rock and began to break up. A lifeboat was launched and twenty passengers managed to scramble into it, but it overturned and all aboard were drowned. A newspaper report described the terrible sounds of the ship's hull thumping against the rock and the 'screams of alarm from the affrighted passengers'. In spite of this, the other lifeboats were launched and the rest of the crew and passengers made it safely ashore. Behind them, the *Sirius* was crunched and rolled until she broke into pieces and sank. That was the end of the heroic steamship.

· ·

EXPLORE THE STORY

Near **Passage West** there is a piece of a ship on display at the waterside. It is part of the paddle shaft of the SS *Sirius*. The museum in Passage West tells the story of the ship.

The *Sirius's* **figurehead** is on display in Hull Maritime Museum, England.

The very fine **tomb of Lieutenant Roberts** is in the churchyard of St Mary's Church of Ireland in Passage West. It records his 'undaunted bravery' and 'consummate skill' as a sailor.

After the loss of the *Sirius*, work began on **Ballycotton lighthouse** as a matter of urgency. It has been safeguarding the coastline where the *Sirius* was wrecked since 1851.

· ·

ILLUSTRATED BY LINDA FAHRLIN

THE STORY OF AN INTREPID MARINE BIOLOGIST

VALENTIA ISLAND IS ONE OF THE MOST WESTERLY POINTS IN ALL OF EUROPE, LOOKING OUT ACROSS THE WATERY HORIZON TOWARDS AMERICA. NOWADAYS, IT IS CONNECTED TO IRELAND BY A ROAD BRIDGE, BUT IN THE 1800S AND EARLY 1900S, IT WAS ACCESSIBLE ONLY BY BOAT. LOOKING OUT ACROSS THE WAVES BACK THEN, YOU MIGHT HAVE BEEN STRUCK BY THE SIGHT OF A SMALL OPEN ROWING BOAT MANNED BY TWO LADIES IN FULL EDWARDIAN DRESS, BOTH OF THEM GAZING FIXEDLY INTO THE WATER, WRITING IN NOTEBOOKS, COLLECTING SAMPLES. WHO WERE THEY AND WHAT WERE THEY DOING?

The Atlantic waters that surge and crash around Valentia Island are very cold and very deep. The island itself is small, about 11 km (7 miles) by 3 km (2 miles), and not heavily populated, but the sea around it is teeming with creatures of every shape, size and description. It was to this island that Maude Delap (1866–1953) moved with her family in 1874, when she was eight years old. One of six hardy sisters, Maude did not get to attend school because she was a girl, and the general opinion was that it wasn't worth paying for a formal education for girls when they weren't going to have a career. Little did they know of Maude Delap!

So, her four brothers headed off to study, but she and her sisters stayed behind and were largely homeschooled. But it didn't matter because when you have an inquiring mind, the whole world is your teacher, from the insects

creeping and buzzing in your garden to the sunrises and sunsets and tides that work their patterns daily. And Maude was an enthusiastic, eagle-eyed and intelligent student.

Her family moved into a big, sea-facing house on the island, called Reenellen. You have to picture a darker, colder time – the house had no electricity, only candles and oil lights, so when night closed in, there was just the turf fire to warm you and the flickering flames of wax and oil to throw some light against the shadows. Back then, people lived closer to the weather and the outdoors, even when behind the walls of their houses. They had to be very aware of the changing sky, learn to read the elements, work the earth to grow food, tend to their animals – it was a very close-to-nature way of life, and Maude revelled in it.

Beyond the front door of Reenellen was a wild place of sea and sky, and it fascinated Maude. She spent hours along the shore, examining the ground beneath her feet. Her sister Constance was just as keen, and together they would push their little rowing boat into the water and explore the sea caves and the harbour, a tow net in hand for gathering up any interesting-looking specimens. This was a very unusual pastime for women in the 1800s, and they must have looked odd setting out in their full skirts and hats, but Maude and her sister didn't care about any of that. Nothing stopped them from doing what they wanted to do.

As her collection of specimens grew, Maude decided she needed more space to do her work. She turned a room in the house into a 'laboratory', where she kept all her books, paraphernalia and jars of marine specimens, all reeking of the salty Atlantic Ocean. She humorously called her work room 'the Department'. Even though other marine biologists had proper university labs and equipment, from this very modest working space Maude made a huge contribution to the international study of marine life. She was before her time, but she forced her time to keep up with her!

***

Have you ever stood over the remains of a jellyfish on the beach, prodding it with your fishing net, wondering how a big lump of quivering jelly can be alive and swim? Well, Maude had the same wonder, and she realized there was a lot to learn about the lives of these strange creatures. She had questions no one could answer. Only one thing for it, then – she captured some jellyfish, kept them in a bell jar in the Department and then charted their life cycle, from breeding to birth to maturity. No one had ever bred jellyfish in captivity before, and Maude's observations and papers on the subject brought brand-new knowledge to marine science.

Maude did lots of fieldwork with Constance, out in the salt-spray wind, sturdy boots on, eyes scanning for anything of interest. You can imagine their absolute delight when Valentia harbour was chosen in the 1890s for a detailed marine study. This meant that a group of naturalists from University College London would set up in Valentia and carry out a scientific survey. Naturally, they wanted the help of the local experts – heaven for the two sisters!

There were two reasons that Valentia was a good choice. The work already carried out by Reverend Delap, the girls' father, and also by Constance and Maude, gave the team a good head start. And then there was the transatlantic telegraph station, observatory and weather station. The island might have been out on its own in the Atlantic, but it was very well connected to the rest of the world because of the transatlantic cable. Maude was lucky to have ended up living on an island that was perfect for studying undisturbed natural habitats but was also at the heart of a very early worldwide web of communications.

***

The cable is a story in itself, and no doubt Maude loved to hear about it once she was old enough to understand. How did you send a message to America or anywhere else beyond Ireland in the 1800s? Very slowly, is the answer. It took weeks to get a simple message across the Atlantic because it had to be taken in a post bag on a boat. There was no such thing as instant communication! That's how the incredible idea of a cable right across the ocean was born.

One ship set out from Ireland and one set out from Canada, with the plan of meeting halfway and joining the two cables, then laying them as they sailed for home. There were many frustrating attempts when the cable snapped, but finally, in 1866, the full cable was laid along the seabed, connecting Valentia to Newfoundland. Now, the telegraph station in Valentia could tap out a message that would be received thousands of miles away – not instantly, but pretty quickly. It was a stunning achievement.

***

The marine scientists came to Valentia in 1895 and immersed themselves in their work on the Valentia Harbour Survey. They were led by Professor Edward T. Browne, whom Maude fell in love with. Unfortunately, he didn't

fall in love with her, and went on to marry another woman. But Maude didn't make a fuss – she continued to send him letters and specimens and sketches of her finds until he died, in 1937.

Her work on the marine survey impressed everyone and Maude was offered a job in Plymouth, England, to work in the marine biological station there. It must have been an amazing moment for Maude. Here she was, a self-taught woman, the island her entire world, and these highly educated men wanted her to come and work with them, to have her own recognized career, to do the work she so loved and receive a salary for it!

But that's not how her story ends. Apparently, when Maude told her father of this wonderful opportunity, he said that the only way a daughter of his would leave home was as a married woman. That was that. Maude couldn't marry her love, and wasn't prepared to give over her time and energy to minding house for a husband, so she had to let that life-changing job go. No one knows what her reply to her father was, but whatever she thought or felt, she simply threw herself deeper into her work and her life on Valentia.

There were wonderful finds to sustain her. One day, a True's beaked whale washed up on the shore – a rare occurrence. She sent a letter to the Natural History Museum in Dublin, and they asked her to chop off the head and flippers and send them to the museum. Undaunted, Maude did as asked – although who knows how she convinced the postman to transport her smelly cut-offs to Dublin! She buried the rest of the whale in the garden at Reenellen. Then, sometime later, the museum wrote again: Please could you send us the bones? Maude rolled up her sleeves and excavated her garden, retrieving the bones and sending them off.

Maude dedicated her whole life to studying marine biology and was unusual in having scientific papers published under her own name in her lifetime. She was also very unusual in having a sea anemone named after her: *Edwardsia delapiae*. She had first discovered it among the eelgrass along the island's shore. For a woman of her time, these were huge achievements – and an excellent example of the importance of following your heart, finding your passion and doing what you love.

EXPLORE THE STORY

You can drive across to **Valentia Island** these days and see its beauty for yourself. **Reenellen** is a derelict old building now, but you can imagine Maud hard at work in 'The Department'.

You can also visit Maude's grave, where she is buried next to her sisters in a little graveyard near **Knightstown**.

You can see the **Transatlantic Cable Station** and some of the original houses of the station workers, in Knightstown.

ILLUSTRATED BY ERIN BROWN

THE STORY OF A LONG AND GRUMPY OLYMPIC GAMES

I N 1906 THE GREAT VOLCANO OF MOUNT VESUVIUS IN ITALY WAS RESTLESS. THE LOCAL PEOPLE WEREN'T WORRIED. THEY WERE USED TO THE MOUNTAIN GRUMBLING AWAY IN THE BACKGROUND. BUT ON THE NIGHT OF 5 APRIL, THEY WERE GREETED BY A VERY WORRYING SIGHT: THE CRATER WAS GLOWING WITH FIRE. THE ERUPTION WHEN IT CAME, WAS DEAFENING, SHOOTING A FIRE STREAM HIGH INTO THE SKY. ASH, FIRE AND ROCKS RAINED DOWN ON NAPLES AND NEARBY VILLAGES, AND ONE HUNDRED PEOPLE WERE KILLED. THE LOCAL PEOPLE COULDN'T HAVE FORESEEN THAT THE EVENTS OF THAT TERRIBLE NIGHT WOULD LEAD TO A VERY MEMORABLE SUMMER OLYMPICS.

The first modern Olympic Games were held in Athens in 1896, but women weren't allowed to take part until 1900. And even then, they could only take part in certain sports that were seen as 'suitable' for ladies, such as croquet and golf. Women athletes had to be well covered, preferably in long dresses, so they could only play sports that allowed for this. Although 'allowed for this' is a bit of a stretch when you see pictures of the women playing tennis in leg-catching long skirts!

At the 1904 Games, archery was added for women. This was a very popular sport, and there was huge interest in the event as athletes got ready for the 1908 Olympics in Rome. But then the volcano erupted. Italy had to put all its energy and money into rebuilding the areas that Vesuvius had streamed lava into, so the organizers needed a new host – and they needed it fast, because the Games were only two years away.

In stepped Britain, happy to take on the challenge of preparing for the Olympics in double-quick time. A new stadium was built at Shepherd's Bush in London that would host almost all of the sports in one place. It was called the White City.

The Games were run very differently back then. They started on 27 April and ended on – wait for it! – 31 October. In fact, this was the longest Games ever held – one of the many firsts that occurred at the 1908 event. There were over 2,000 athletes from twenty-two nations, including thirty-seven female athletes, and this was the first time everyone had to compete as part of a national team. And another first – as there were national teams, it was decided that during the opening ceremony, the athletes would march behind their national flag and pay their respects to King Edward VII in the royal box. Well, that was when the difficulties started.

First off, Britain said that Irish athletes had to compete under the United Kingdom flag. Some of the athletes were happy to do this, others were not.

As a competitor in archery, Beatrice Hill-Lowe came under this rule. She was an Irishwoman, born in Ardee, County Louth, but as Ireland was then part of the United Kingdom of Great Britain and Ireland, Hill-Lowe had a choice to make: compete as part of Team GB or not compete at all. There is not much known about her, so her thoughts on the matter were never recorded, but she was married to an Englishman and had made England her home, so she might not have minded this ruling too much. Whatever her opinion, Hill-Lowe was anxious to compete in archery at Olympic level and she signed up.

The funny thing was, in spite of there being twenty-two nations represented in the Games, only one nation entered women in the archery event. Every single one of the twenty-five competitors were under the United Kingdom flag, so the results look most odd to our eyes, with a long, unbroken line of Union Jacks in the archery results. That's one way to sweep the boards!

There was another problem, though. The US team were feeling a little annoyed with how the Games were being conducted. For one, when they got to the stadium, they saw the flags of the twenty-two nations proudly flying around the roof – except there were two missing, the American and Swedish. The British claimed they couldn't find them. Well, at least the Americans had brought their own for the flag ceremony – so that was fine, wasn't it? Not entirely. The other rule was that during the flag ceremony, each flag-bearer had to dip their country's flag towards the king, as a mark of respect. There were some athletes on the American team with strong opinions about this.

Team USA featured a large number of Irish-born men, including Matthew McGrath, who held the world record for the hammer throw. The other nations paraded past and dipped their flags, but the story goes that McGrath warned the US flag-bearer, Ralph Rose, not to lower the flag. The flag remained stubbornly upright as they passed the royal box, and the people of Britain were outraged. It might have caused a row back then, but this eventually became the code of the US Olympic team, and to this day the American flag-bearer never dips the flag 'to any person or any thing'.

After all that furore, the Games finally got underway and people could enjoy the spectacle. In another first, this was the first time the Games were filmed, so we can watch footage of some of the events. It all looks very different from what we are used to today. The tug-o-war was included in 1908, for the first and last time. The officials look very dapper in their hats and moustaches. There's a very casual air, with people milling about and some sitting on the grass like picnickers, watching the events take place around them.

The women's archery event is included in the film footage, and there is Beatrice Hill-Lowe, concentrating intently, looking the height of fashion in her waist-cinching corset and long skirt, her bows hanging in an array from her waist. The women competed in a double national round, hitting targets fifty and sixty yards away. Hill-Lowe had stiff competition to face down. The favourite was Sybil Fenton 'Queenie' Newell, an experienced archer, and Charlotte 'Lottie' Dod was tipped for great things too.

The archery event took place over two days, and at the end there was a gold medal for Newell, a silver for Dod, and Hill-Lowe won the bronze. This makes Hill-Lowe the first Irishwoman to ever win an Olympic medal, which is an historic achievement. And it wasn't the only one that day, because Newell became – and remains – the oldest woman to ever win an Olympic medal. She was fifty-three years old when she shot her way to victory.

There was one other dramatic moment in London that became a famous part of Games history. King Edward let it be known that he wanted the marathon to begin at Windsor Castle, so his grandchildren could witness the start of the race. And the organizers wanted to finish the race in front of the royal box, adding another 195 m (0.1 miles) at that end. So now they were expected to run 42.195 km (26.2 miles) – and every metre matters when you're running for a couple of hours! The marathon distance had shifted about during the various Games, but from 1924 the 1908 distance became the standard Olympic marathon.

A total of seventy-five runners took off from Windsor Castle, and the first to reach White City was the Italian competitor, pastry chef Dorando Pietri. But the run had taken a toll on Pietri and he veered wildly once in the stadium, setting off in the wrong direction around the track. The crowd watched, hearts in mouths, as he staggered towards the finish line and then collapsed to the ground. The race officials had to prop him back up on his feet. The crowd cheered him onwards and he finally made it over the line. But his winning moment soon turned sour when he was disqualified for receiving help to finish the race. What a terrible blow after all that hard work! The royals obviously felt very sorry for him because Queen Alexandra presented him with a gold cup to mark his achievement – and make up a little bit for losing out on a gold medal.

It had been an entertaining and controversial Olympic Games, from start to finish. It's sad that we don't have any record of Beatrice Hill-Lowe's reaction to her win, or to the various arguments that flared up around the Games. Was she so focused on her own performance that it all passed her by? Or were the athletes following the dramatic moments with great interest and curiosity? And did she have a proud sense of what she had done – the first Irishwoman to win a medal, ensuring her place in Irish history? And did she realize that the Irish-born competitors won a staggering twenty-three medals between them in those Games? We just don't know.

EXPLORE THE STORY

You can see the actual Bronze Olympic medal presented to Beatrice Hill-Lowe in 1908 at the **County Museum, Dundalk**, County Louth.

On **YouTube**, you can search for London 1908 Olympic Games and view the footage filmed during the Games.

ILLUSTRATED BY DONOUGH O'MALLEY

THE STORY OF THE U-BOAT AND THE GUINNESS SHIP

ORLD WAR I RAGED FROM 1914 TO 1918, A TIME WHEN IRELAND WAS STILL PART OF THE BRITISH EMPIRE. IN ALL, AROUND 200,000 IRISH MEN ENLISTED IN THE BRITISH, CANADIAN AND AMERICAN ARMIES, AND ABOUT 30,000 IRISH PEOPLE LOST THEIR LIVES IN THE FIGHTING IN EUROPE. BUT THE WAR WAS ALSO FOUGHT MUCH, MUCH CLOSER TO HOME. THE GERMAN NAVY SAW THE IRISH SEA AS PART OF THE 'THEATRE OF WAR', AND THEIR U-BOATS, OR SUBMARINES, HAUNTED THESE WATERS, REGARDING EVERY VESSEL AS 'THE ENEMY'. STEPPING ONTO A SHIP – EVEN IF IT WAS JUST A MERCHANT SHIP OR A MAIL BOAT – WAS HIGHLY DANGEROUS. NO ONE WAS SAFE.

On 7 May 1915, the massive *Lusitania* passenger liner was sailing from New York to Liverpool. It was the biggest ship in the world when it was launched in 1906 and was the last word in luxury travel. On this voyage, it was thronged with passengers, all enjoying the chance to experience a transatlantic crossing like no other.

The beautiful liner had made its way right across the Atlantic without incident. It was sailing majestically past the Old Head of Kinsale in County Cork when, unknown to everyone on board, it was sighted by a lurking U-20, a silent and deadly German submarine.

The U-boat fired a single torpedo and scored a direct hit. Incredibly, the huge ship took just eighteen minutes to sink beneath the waves. The death toll was terrible – 1,198 passengers and crew drowned in the deep waters, with around 764 managing to get into lifeboats and live to tell the tale. For days afterwards, bodies of the drowned washed up on the shore and were buried in mass graves in Cobh. Many others were lost forever because the waves didn't return their bodies at all. There had never been an attack of this scale before, and it shocked everyone, from Ireland all the way to America.

It was very clear that the war was on water now, as well as on land, and every vessel in Irish waters was a target. Over the next few years, the U-boats would claim a huge number of ships. They torpedoed some, shelled others, and also planted mines, moored below the surface of the water, that were hard to detect and devastating upon impact. The corridor of sea between Ireland and Britain became known as the 'killing lanes', and it took a brave soul to venture forth onto that stretch of open water.

The *W.M. Barkley* was the proud flagship of the Guinness brewery in Dublin – the first vessel of what would become a small working fleet. As the very first Guinness merchant ship, the *W.M. Barkley* sailed back and forth between Britain and Ireland, delivering barrels of stout to the thirsty people across the Irish Sea. That's exactly what it was doing on 12 October 1917 – bringing a cargo of Guinness across to Liverpool. The steam ship left Dublin Port at about 5 p.m. and headed out onto the choppy waves.

The ship wasn't totally defenceless. In fact, it was the first Irish merchant ship to have a gun mounted on the deck and a gunner to man it. But perhaps the thirteen crew members thought themselves safe – after all, what harm could Guinness pose to the German navy? There was no reason to attack a merchant ship and blow up barrels of stout – what good would that do anyone? They'd be better off stopping the ship and stealing the cargo and enjoying it!

That might be what the crew hoped, but if they did, they were wrong. Deep in the cold, dark water of the Irish Sea, completely unseen by the crew of the *W.M. Barkley*, a UC-75 submarine was lying in wait. When it spotted the merchant ship, there was no hesitation. Captain Johannes Lohs gave the order, as he had so many times before.

Fire!

A torpedo was unleashed, slicing through the water, dead on target. It hit the steam ship, which immediately began to take on water. It would have been over very quickly if it wasn't for the cargo of barrels. Incredibly, it was the barrels of Guinness that kept the ship afloat long enough for the crew to launch a lifeboat. You might be wondering about the gun on deck at this point, and the gunner – why didn't the ship fire off some shots and defend itself, or try to inflict some damage on the attacker? There was one slight problem. While the U-boat was preparing to torpedo the ship, the gunner was down in the galley (kitchen) doing a bit of washing up. Not exactly a model of readiness!

Five crewmen died in the explosion, but the other eight managed to escape. One of those was a man called Thomas McGlue. He was later interviewed by Guinness and gave an extraordinary first-hand account of what had happened to the *W.M. Barkley* that night.

When the torpedo hit, McGlue said he was 'in the galley, aft of the bridge. I was just reaching out to take a kettle off the fire to make a cup of tea for the officers. When we got the poke [torpedo hit], the kettle capsized and shot the boiling water up my arm to the elbow.'

Even though he was injured and in pain, McGlue managed to cut the lifeboat free and jumped into it, along with his crewmates. They looked around and saw the cause of their distress close by, looking back at them:

There were seven Germans in the conning tower, all looking down at us through binoculars.

We hailed the captain and asked him to pick us up. He called us alongside and then asked us the name of our boat, the cargo she was carrying, how the owners were, where she was registered, and where she was bound to. He spoke better English than we did. We answered his questions and then asked if we could go.

He told us to wait a minute while he went below and checked the name on the register. Then he came back up again and said, 'I can't find her'. He went back three times altogether. Then he came back and said, 'All right we've found her and ticked her off.'

... Then he pointed out the shore lights and told us to steer for them. The submarine slipped away and we were left alone, with hogsheads of

stout bobbing all around us. The Barkley had broken and gone down very quietly. We tried to row for the Kish light vessel, but it might have been America for all the way we made.

We got tired and my scalded hand was hurting. We put out the sea anchor and sat there shouting all night.

The lucky crew members were eventually rescued and made it back alive. It's thought there are about 1,800 ships in the waters around Ireland dating to the war years, among them around fifteen U-boats. These wrecks lying on the seabed, being slowly eaten by tide and time, are the silent keepers of the terrifying tales of the war at sea. Imagine what they could tell us, if only they could speak. Well, now there is a way for them to give up their stories.

***

Have you ever heard tell of an underwater archaeologist? Doesn't that just sound like the best job in the world! In Ireland, there is an Underwater Archaeological Unit (UAU) that finds, records, maps and dives on wrecks in Irish waters in order to find out the stories they have to tell. They have to figure out where the wrecks might lie on the seabed, use special equipment to locate them and then dive down to those wrecks to gather information, take photographs and make detailed sketches. They work with the Irish National Seabed Survey (INSS) and the INFOMAR mapping project to create a huge database of all the wrecked vessels – a task that will take a long time to complete.

The *W.M. Barkley* has already been found by the survey. It lies east of Howth Head, in water about 56 m (184 ft) deep, and the bow (front) of the ship lies separate from the rest, showing how the torpedo cut through the wooden vessel. The archaeologists have captured images of the ship in its sorry state on the seabed, but it is quite hard to see. In time, it will break up completely and be no more. That's why the work of underwater archaeology is so important – because it preserves the information for future generations who won't have the actual wreck to examine any more.

There is one part of the story of the *W.M. Barkley* that not even the underwater archaeologists can shed light on, though. The cargo of Guinness floated away on the waves, with reports of barrels washing up along Ireland's east coast and Britain's west coast. Wherever did those barrels go?

EXPLORE THE STORY

At the **Guinness Storehouse** in Dublin, there is a Transport Gallery and it has a scale model of the *W.M. Barkley*.

If you do like the sound of underwater archaeology, check out **www.archaeology.ie** for more information on the UAU of the National Monuments Service, Ireland.

ILLUSTRATED BY LYDIA HUGHES

THE STORY OF THE ORIGINAL GRAND PRIX

CAN YOU PICTURE A FORMULA ONE RACE BEING HELD IN IRELAND? BETTER STILL, CAN YOU PICTURE IT BEING HELD ON IRISH ROADS? IT'S VERY HARD TO IMAGINE LEWIS HAMILTON CAREENING AROUND THE BACKROADS, DODGING POTHOLES AND CHICKENS IN HIS QUEST FOR GLORY! SO IT MIGHT COME AS A SURPRISE TO LEARN THAT THE ORIGINS OF THE GRAND PRIX CAN BE TRACED ALL THE WAY BACK TO THE BOREENS AROUND COUNTY KILDARE – HONESTLY!

It was 29 April 1899, and Belgian engineer Camille Jenatzy was sitting in the car he had built with his own hands, eager to break records. He had been chasing a speed record for the past year, vying with his great rival, and his new car might just be the one to finally do it. He had built the car in the shape of a bullet, with a seat high up, perched on four small wheels. It looked like he was sitting inside a mini torpedo – and he hoped it would have the same ballistic force. He called his electric car La Jamais Contente – 'The Never Satisfied'. It was a good name too for the man himself, who was always involved in some fast-paced adventure in his beloved cars, never content, always eager to leap forward with the next crazy idea.

The car took off, Jenatzy at the wheel, willing it on to ever greater speeds. The batteries pumped, the electric motors raced and for a glorious 1.2 km (0.75 miles) Jenatzy's bullet car hit 105.9 kmph (65.8 mph). That was it! He had done it! The first person in the history of car driving to break 100 kmph (62 mph). It was exhilarating – and addictive.

***

In Paris, there was another wild adventurer who would end up giving Jenatzy the opportunity to compete in thrilling high-speed races. James Gordon Bennett was a bit like Camille Jenatzy in that he was always up for adventure of any kind. He was born into a very wealthy New York family. His father had founded the *New York Herald* newspaper, while his mother was a music teacher from County Meath called Henrietta Crean. Her son lived a privileged life of sailing yachts and luxury and hijinks. He was a handsome young man and made a good match as husband to an equally wealthy young woman. Things did not go according to plan, however, thanks to his wild streak. He turned up to a party thrown by the family of his wife-to-be after visiting a pub on the way. His behaviour fell far, far below what was expected. (Let's just say he mistook the grand piano for the loo!) The young lady's brother challenged him to a duel, intending to punish him for offending his sister, but luckily for Bennett, they both missed their target. It was time for the wild young Bennett to make a change – he agreed to move to Paris and run his family's newspaper interests there. You can imagine that his family might have been relieved to wave him off!

Bennett adored sports of all kinds and setting up competitions and races. He also adored motor cars. His passions came together when he set up the Gordon Bennett Cup race. The first was in 1900, and the cars raced from Paris to Dijon. It was a great success, and races were held in 1901 and 1902, both times racing between European cities. In 1902, the English competitor, Selwyn Edge, beat the whole field, much to everyone's surprise because the French contenders were thought to be unbeatable. The rule stated that the winner must host the following year's competition. There was a problem, though: motor racing was not allowed in the UK, and they didn't really like the idea of a noisy, dangerous race taking over the roads. Someone hit on a bright idea: why not hold it in Ireland and lift the motor racing ban *there*? (In 1903, Ireland was still part of the United Kingdom.) Hey presto – problem solved!

At that time, there were about 250 motor cars in the whole of Ireland – a rare sight. That was about to change. Once the race was set, there was huge excitement. It would be the biggest sporting event ever held in the country and everyone wanted to see it. Twelve racers signed up to take part – from the UK, France, Germany and the USA. They each had a country colour for their cars, and to honour the fact that the race was taking place in Ireland, the British competitor chose emerald green. That's how British racing green was first created.

The other cup races had been city-to-city, but this one was a closed circuit, racing laps in a figure-of-eight through Athy and around many towns and villages. By the time the racers had completed all of the many laps, they would have raced a staggering 527 km (327.5 miles).

There was a 19 kmph (12 mph) speed limit for all Irish roads, but this was changed for the race day so they could put their cars to the test. However, they had to stick to the speed limit going through the villages, for everyone's safety. Every car had to travel behind a bicycle to make sure it was travelling slow enough. It must have been very hard to go from full-throttle, heart-racing speeds to suddenly braking and crawling through the towns and villages. It wouldn't do your nerves any good!

On 2 July, the cars made their way to the start line at Ballyshannon, County Kildare, and the spectators looked on eagerly, impatient for the big race to take off. These unpredictable races had become very dangerous, for drivers and spectators, but Ireland did an excellent job, putting 2,000 police officers to work as stewards to ensure it ran smoothly. Thousands of people thronged the route, all looking to see what these racing cars were all about.

In the German Mercedes car sat Camille Jenatzy, blood fizzing in his veins as he waited for his signal to go go go. It was all set. Each car would leave seven minutes after the one ahead, to try to avoid collisions. Time to give the signal.

And they're off!

Twelve cars hared off around the course, which brought them through Kildare, Laois and Carlow. The had to navigate bumps, bends and boisterous crowds as they went. One competitor, Englishman Charles Jarrott, described later how he seemed to meet as many chickens as people on those roads. It was harum-scarum stuff, not for the faint-hearted. In the end, only five cars were left in the race. The others had all broken down or suffered punctures or crashed – or, in the case of Selwyn Edge, had been disqualified. The previous year's winner was disqualified because locals in Athy had thrown buckets of water over his tyres to cool them

down. That was classified as receiving assistance to win, which wasn't allowed.

There could only be one winner, of course. And after six hours and thirty-nine minutes, Camille Jenatzy's Mercedes car crossed the line – and took the cup! He had averaged a speed of 79.1 kmph (49.2 mph) to clinch the title. Not quite Lewis Hamilton speed, but it was enough to take the title on the day. He had won the Gordon Bennett Cup!

The man himself, Gordon Bennett, withdrew his sponsorship of the race in 1905, but it was already established and went on without him. Bennett continued to enjoy his unusual and luxurious life. Apparently, his Mediterranean yacht included two cows on the crew – to provide him with the freshest milk possible, even when he was drifting far from shore!

***

As for Jenatzy, he died as he had lived – a bit crazily! You might expect that he ended up in a car smash, given his love of speed, but he died of a prank gone wrong. It wasn't a very well-thought-out prank, to be fair. It is reported that he was on a shooting trip with friends and came up with a genius idea to give them a fright. He left them enjoying their evening drinks, went outside, wedged himself behind a bush and proceeded to give a stirring performance of a wild boar in full throat. It was so convincing, one of the guests poked his head out the window, then shot at the bush – killing the 'wild boar' stone dead. Poor Jenatzy. After all that wonderful hell-raising and adventuring, he made himself quarry for a hunter. What an ending to his story!

EXPLORE THE STORY
The **Gordon Bennett Classic Car Rally** is held every year around County Kildare and the original closed circuit of the 1903 race.

ILLUSTRATED BY ÚNA WOODS

THE STORY OF A GLASS CEILING AND TWO HAMMERS

IT'S HARD FOR US TO THINK OF IT NOW – THANKFULLY! – BUT ONLY A HUNDRED YEARS AGO WOMEN'S LIVES WERE VERY DIFFERENT. IT REALLY WAS A MAN'S WORLD, AND WOMEN OFTEN GOT THE RAW END OF THE DEAL. THEY WORKED HARD, RAISED FAMILIES, SUPPORTED THEIR HUSBANDS, BROTHERS AND FATHERS AND CONTRIBUTED MUCH TO SOCIETY, YET THEY COULDN'T VOTE, THEY COULDN'T EASILY ACCESS EDUCATION AND MANY JOBS WERE BARRED TO THEM. HOW DID WOMEN BREAK THROUGH THIS THICK GLASS CEILING? WELL, IT WAS A COMBINATION OF THINGS COMING TOGETHER TO FINALLY GIVE THEM THEIR CHANCE.

Averil Deverell and Frances Kyle will always have a place in the history books as the first women in Britain and Ireland to become barristers. They were both born in the nineteenth century, in 1893, and they both died in the twentieth century, so they got to live through one of the most interesting and fast-moving periods in women's history. The last hundred years have changed women's lives completely, and we have pioneering women like Averil and Frances to thank for that.

There was a very big 'before' and 'after' in Averil's life – and it echoes a much bigger before and after for women as well. In 1911, she was presented at Court. This meant dressing in an extremely beautiful white dress, with a full train and gloves, and meeting King George V and Queen Mary in the Throne Room at Dublin Castle. This was a ceremony for wealthy young women, or those whose parents were connected with the royal family in some way. In Averil's case, her father was clerk of the Crown and peace for County Wicklow. The reason why George V was sitting on a throne in Dublin was that, in 1911, Ireland was still a part of the United Kingdom and had been since 1801. It is unlikely anyone present at Averil's big royal evening would have guessed that the world they had grown up in was about to change forever.

The first female student had been admitted to Trinity College Dublin in 1904, and with her background, Averil was able to get a place there, studying law, alongside her brother. However, unlike her brother, Averil would not be able to work as a solicitor or a barrister because women were not allowed to join those professions. Many people saw the education of women as a waste of time anyway – they were only going to end up at home, having babies and sewing things. What else could they do?

An awful lot was the answer.

There's an old saying: 'It's an ill wind that blows no good', and that could be said of the outbreak of World War I in 1914. It was a terrible war, and it is estimated that by the time it ended, 40 million people had lost their lives. That's a staggering loss of life. It changed the world. But in doing so, it also changed the world for women. At first, they were told to stay home and help out by rationing or growing food or darning socks – nice, easy tasks. But as the years ground on and more and more men were dragged into the war machine, it became clear that women had to be let into other areas of work.

Over in Ireland, Averil Deverell graduated from Trinity College in 1915 and then helped the war effort by serving as a nursing sister. In 1918, she somehow persuaded the British authorities to let her go to France as an ambulance driver. She was obviously a woman determined to follow her own path!

There have been millions of words written about World War I and its history, but the fact that thousands of women volunteered as ambulance drivers on the front line isn't perhaps as well known as it should be. At the start of the war, many men would have been outright shocked at the idea of a woman driver – cars were pretty new things then, let alone women driving them! But as the war went on and the women proved themselves to be brave, skilful drivers and handy mechanics, able to defrost an engine or change a tyre as well as anyone, the men eventually had to acknowledge that women were excellent allies.

This experience meant that Averil had already broken one glass ceiling in her life – and no doubt she had some extraordinary experiences on the front line. And, of course, she must have been good at ducking and dodging bullets because she survived.

After the war, women weren't willing to go back to the old traditional roles. Both women and men had seen a new way of doing things, had seen first-hand how they could work together and how reliable women were, and that paved the way for some long-awaited progress. The war ended in 1918, and no one could turn back the clock and pretend it hadn't happened, least of all the brave women who had volunteered and served their time. They were capable of so much, and they wanted to do more.

This wind of change led to the Sex Disqualification (Removal) Act 1919, which was an extraordinary moment in women's history. Up until then, there were a lot of jobs women were not allowed to do – they could not become barristers, vets, judges or civil servants, for example. They weren't allowed to do those jobs simply because they were women – that was the only reason, and it was a silly reason. But this new law said that they could no longer be blocked from these professions and that they had to be given a fair chance.

Well, that was all Averil Deverell and Frances Kyle needed to hear. They didn't know each other, but in 1920 each woman signed up to King's Inns, Ireland's oldest school of law, where they studied to become barristers. They were the very first female students admitted there, and they were both quite brilliant students. Frances came first in her class, while Averil had a reputation for being hard-working and witty. Given their brains and ability, they easily passed their exams – and then came the historic day.

On 1 November 1921, these two women graduated as barristers-at-law. They had taken a lump hammer to the glass ceiling and smashed a way through for all women. These two were the first female barristers in Britain or Ireland. It was such a huge moment for the legal profession that they made headlines around the world. Their photos appeared in the *New York Times* and the *Times of India*. If it was today, they'd be trending on Twitter and smashing it on TikTok!

It can't have been easy for these two first women – they would have been the only women in the room most of the time, with only male colleagues around them, and they would have had to constantly to prove to everyone they met that they could do the job well. In fact, Frances did wonder if she would be able to make a living, if clients would be willing to have a woman as their barrister. But she knew that being a trailblazer wasn't going to be easy – that, in many ways, blazing the trail was itself the most important thing. She lit the way for other women coming behind her.

Averil enjoyed a long and respected career over the next forty years. She was the first Irish woman barrister to appear before the Privy Council in London, which is a big deal in legal circles and earned her the right to carry the 'red bag'. Barristers carried their legal documents for their cases in a 'brief bag'. The normal bag was blue, but a red bag was given as a special gift, to mark the fact that this person was particularly excellent at their job. Averil's red brief bag marked her out as a really, really good barrister.

It can be hard to be the first at something; it means you have no one to guide you or to show you how it's done. That's why Averil Deverell and Frances Kyle are so important – they showed that it was possible, and that women could work alongside men in any job. And that they could be brilliant at it! They are women of history and deserve to be remembered and celebrated.

EXPLORE THE STORY

A portrait of Averil Deverell hangs in the **Law Library** in the Four Courts in Dublin. In the portrait she has her red brief-bag with her – now you'll be able to explain why it matters! A plaque next to the portraits records: 'Miss Averil Deverell. Called to The Bar of Ireland 1st November, 1921. She was with, Miss F.C. Kyle, the first Lady to be called to the Irish Bar, and was called prior to the admission of any lady to the English Bar.'

ILLUSTRATED BY EVA BYRNE

THE STORY OF PADDY THE PIGEON, DECORATED WAR HERO

NOAH BUILT THE ARK, ACCORDING TO THE BIBLICAL STORY, AND THEN THE RAIN STARTED TO FALL. IT RAINED AND RAINED AND RAINED. THE WHOLE WORLD FILLED UP WITH WATER, WHILE NOAH AND HIS PAIRS OF ANIMALS FLOATED ALONG, NOT KNOWING WHEN THE FLOODS WOULD EBB AWAY – OR WHERE THEY'D END UP. THE MOMENT OF JOY CAME WHEN NOAH SENT OUT A DOVE AND IT CAME BACK TO THE ARK CARRYING AN OLIVE BRANCH IN ITS BEAK. IT HAD FOUND LAND – LIFE! SINCE THEN, THE DOVE AND PIGEON HAVE BEEN THE MESSENGERS OF HOPE. SO, PADDY THE PIGEON COMES FROM A LONG LINE OF LIFESAVERS, WHO BRING HOPE JUST WHEN IT'S NEEDED MOST.

Pigeons are found right across the world and are often seen as pesky nuisances who hoover up any food going and poop it all back out over cars, paths and sometimes people. It's said to be lucky if a bird poops on you, but it never feels that way! Pigeons are so common, it's easy to overlook their incredible history as messengers. Did you know that they were prized as allies in both world wars? One US army major remarked to the New York Times that 'pigeons can win battles'. He wasn't joking.

Pigeoneers were an important part of the fighting forces in World War I. A pigeoneer is a pigeon trainer, particularly one who trains homing pigeons for use in military operations. They have to start the training at about four weeks old, before they have coded their birth loft as 'home', which is thought to happen at around six weeks. The pigeoneer has to catch the pigeon young if the training is to be a success.

Once the pigeon is bonded to 'home', they will return to it from great distances. We now know that they navigate by using the Earth's magnetic field. Humans don't have this ability, but many birds do, and pigeons are particularly good at it. That's why you can drop them hundreds of miles from home and they can find their way back. The American pigeoneers found this out when training a homing pigeon called Chester. He was released as part of a training group from the US army base at Fort Meade. All of the other birds made it back that evening, but there was no sign of Chester. He was given up as lost. But the following day, a soldier making his way to the camp saw a strange sight. There was Chester, his wings covered in oil and useless for flight, plodding tiredly down the road leading to Fort Meade. Fly or walk, Chester was going home.

It was this dogged reliability that made pigeons so valuable in war time. In World War I, over 100,000 pigeons were put to work. Someone came up with the ingenious idea of mobile lofts – in other words, pigeon homes on wheels. This made it much easier to use the pigeons' incredible homing instincts. Things like double-decker buses were converted into lofts, so the pigeons' home could be moved around and they didn't have to cover such huge distances. On the German side, they even had pigeons with little cameras strapped to their bellies, turning them into aerial photographers!

So, when World War II broke out, the Allies knew full well how crucial the pigeon corps could be. In all, about 200,000 pigeons were pressed into service by the British army, and they proved themselves time and time again. The British could send messages to Resistance fighters in France, for example, asking for information on German movements. They simply attached a little metal tube to the bird's leg, pushed a rolled-up piece of paper inside and there you had it, a reliable, speedy postal service that could swoop behind enemy lines – and maybe even poop on their heads!

The pigeon personnel were so effective, the German army had to find ways to try to stop them. When gunners spotted pigeons in flight, they didn't wait to find out if they were carrying a little metal tube, they shot them out of the sky – if their marksman skills were good enough. They also developed their own set of fighter birds – falcons and hawks. These were released to patrol the skies, attacking any pigeon they laid their beady eyes on. There was human war on the ground and bird war in the skies above.

Among this huge battalion of pigeons, some stood out – and none more so than Paddy. He had hatched in Carnlough, County Antrim. His owner, Andrew Hughes, trained him as a messenger pigeon and then gave him to the National Pigeon Service, to be trained to work with the British army. After a very successful training stint with the RAF at their Hurn air base, Paddy was promoted to carry out the most dangerous, most valuable messenger job: to carry coded information about the Allies' advances and movements during the Normandy landings and bring it back to England.

The D-Day landings took place on 6 June 1944, and it was a huge turning point in the long war. It was the largest seaborne attack in history: over 5,000 ships and boats landing about 150,000 troops on the beaches of southwest France. This was the moment when the Allies needed to defeat the German war machine. The attack would take place by sea, air and land all at the same time, pushing the German defences to the limit. It could be the counterattack that would end the war and secure victory – but that would require a good flow of information to keep the troops working together and moving safely.

That was where Paddy came in. It might seem crazy that this responsibility fell onto the bandy little legs of a pigeon, but that's exactly what happened. The command in Normandy attached a coded message to Paddy's leg and released him. He didn't let them down. Paddy flew straight and true for four hours and fifty minutes, covering the 370 km (230 miles) between Normandy and his home base in

Hampshire. That meant he averaged a speed of 90 kmph (56 mph) all the way – the fastest of all of the messenger pigeons who set off that day.

His ferocious flying, and his ability to dodge falcons, hawks, guns and awful weather, turned Paddy into a hero. He delivered his message in record time, giving essential information to the war planners back in Britain. In the end, D-Day won the battle for the Allies, halting Germany's advance across Europe and, finally, leading to peace.

On 1 September 1944, Paddy was awarded the Dickin Medal in recognition of his bravery and his contribution to the war effort. The Dickin Medal is very special – it is awarded to those animals that display gallantry and devotion to their duty in wartime. So far, thirty-two pigeons have received this honour, but Paddy is the only one from Ireland to do so. It's described as the Victoria Cross of the animal world. The bronze medal is inscribed with the words 'For Gallantry' and 'We Also Serve'.

And who was Dickin, you are no doubt wondering. The medal was established in 1943 by Maria Dickin, who founded the People's Dispensary for Sick Animals (PDSA) in Britain. She wanted to acknowledge the devotion shown by animals and their heroic efforts in helping their humans. To date, seventy-four animals have received the medal – and no doubt many more will be added in time.

Paddy's flight out of Normandy was extraordinary. There were so many things that could have gone wrong – but then, pigeons are known for their resilience. He was lucky to escape

FOR
Gallantry
PADDY
THE
PIDGEON

the fate of some of his feathered friends. After D-Day, the British came up with an ingenious plan to drop pigeons – both alive and dead – all across Germany. The live pigeons would carry questionnaires inviting the German people to inform on their leaders in order to bring the war to an end. The dead pigeons would carry the same questionnaire, but already filled out – apparently by traitorous Germans. They were actually filled out by the British, looking to hoodwink their opponents. You can imagine the reaction at base when one of these live pigeons made it home, with its precious metal tube intact. Inside, the message from a German person read: **Thank you. I had the sister of this one for supper. Delicious. Please send us some more.** That poor pigeon made an even greater sacrifice for the war effort!

After the war, Paddy went home to Carnlough and lived a life of free flying with Andrew Hughes. He died in 1954.

Paddy the Pigeon has not been forgotten. The people of Carnlough erected a plaque in his honour, so that his role in the war would never be forgotten. It records that Paddy flew 'the fastest time recorded by a message-carrying pigeon during the Normandy landings' and that he remains, 'to date … the only Irish recipient of the Dickin Medal'. A fitting tribute for a pigeon that knew no fear!

....

EXPLORE THE STORY
You can see the plaque commemorating Paddy's heroic flight in **Carnlough**, County Antrim.

....

ILLUSTRATED BY LINDA FAHRLIN

THE STORY OF OPERATION HUMPTY DUMPTY

DO YOU REMEMBER THE RHYME FROM WHEN YOU WERE LITTLE? 'HUMPTY DUMPTY SAT ON A WALL. HUMPTY DUMPTY HAD A GREAT FALL. ALL THE KING'S HORSES AND ALL THE KING'S MEN COULDN'T PUT HUMPTY TOGETHER AGAIN.' THERE ARE DIFFERENT IDEAS ABOUT WHAT THE RHYME MEANS. IS IT ABOUT KING RICHARD III, OR IS IT JUST ABOUT AN EGG – WHO KNOWS? WHAT IT DOES SEEM TO REFER TO, THOUGH, IS SOMETHING THAT GETS BROKEN AND CANNOT BE PUT BACK THE WAY IT WAS BEFORE, NO MATTER WHAT EFFORTS ARE MADE. AND THAT CERTAINLY RINGS TRUE FOR THE 'HUMPTY DUMPTY' IN IRISH HISTORY.

There is a famous statue of Admiral Lord Nelson in Trafalgar Square in London, and there used to be another very famous one on Sackville Street (now O'Connell Street) in Dublin. Until 1922, Ireland was part of the British Empire, so famous British leaders ended up as statues on Ireland's streets. The statue of Nelson was the most prominent because it stood on top of a soaring pillar, 36.6 m (120 ft) high, from which the admiral glared over the noisy, bustling street below. That's why it was called Nelson's Pillar.

It was a magnificent structure that drew visitors from far and wide. From the bottom of the pillar to the top of Nelson's head, it stood 40.7 m (133.5 ft) tall, higher than any other building or monument in the area. Best of all, for a ten-pence fee you could go inside the pillar and climb the 168 spiralling stairs up to a viewing platform, from where there were wide and beautiful views across the city, the River Liffey and

Dublin Bay. It was a monument, yes, but it was also a tourist attraction and offered a unique view of Dublin.

The statue had been there since 1809 – so long that most Dubliners probably didn't give much thought anymore to who Nelson was or why he was looking down on them from such a height. When you look at something often enough, you stop seeing it. But after Ireland fought its War of Independence and declared the Irish Free State in 1922, some people began to take a lot more notice of Lord Nelson atop his pillar. And after Ireland was declared a republic in 1949, there were outright arguments and threats. Many people felt that Dublin's grandest thoroughfare should have statues to Irish heroes. Why would a republic have such a huge monument to another country's naval hero? It made no sense. But still Lord Nelson held his place, while far below plots to topple him were hatched and abandoned.

The year 1966 was the fiftieth anniversary of the Easter Rising of 1916 – an event Nelson had witnessed from his perch, when bullets had ricocheted around his pillar as British and Irish forces fought each other on the streets of Dublin. A small group of men decided to make the anniversary spectacular. Liam Sutcliffe offered to plant a bomb on Nelson, and in 2000, Sutcliffe told the story on a radio programme for the first time – that's how we know exactly what happened. They called their daring – and you'd have to say foolhardy – mission Operation Humpty Dumpty. The aim was to ensure that Admiral Lord Nelson had a great fall.

One afternoon around the end of February 1966, Sutcliffe took his three-year-old son on a visit to the viewing platform on Nelson's pillar. In his bag he had a homemade bomb, made from gelignite and ammonal. Imagine that! A bomb. In a bag. How do you know it won't detonate all of a sudden? It was a huge risk. Sutcliffe admitted later that he regretted bringing his son along that day – but he needed the little boy as a decoy, so he wouldn't look suspicious. Well, it worked.

They made it safely to the top and left the bomb there, timed to go off during the night when the pillar was closed and deserted.

What happened next? Nothing. No explosion. Silence. And Lord Nelson was still standing there the next morning, as intact as ever. The bomb had failed to explode! Now there was a live bomb on a public monument in the middle of a busy city centre. There was nothing for it but to go and get it. So, Sutcliffe went back the next morning, climbed the spiral steps again, and retrieved his bag. If planting it there in the first place was scary, coming back down with an overdue explosion in his bag must have been downright petrifying!

He made it home safely. Then he tinkered with the timer and set it once more for a night-time explosion. On 7 March he set out again – alone this time, he didn't risk bringing his son – and went back to leave his bomb with Nelson. He did it just before closing time and was the last to leave the pillar. When he told the story, he recalled how the caretaker had bid him goodnight and how he had said to himself, under his breath, 'You'd better start looking for a new job tomorrow.' He must have been confident he had fixed that timer.

Liam Sutcliffe left the pillar, went home and went to sleep.

The next morning, he got up, got dressed and headed off to work. On the way, he could hear people talking in shock, and the newspapers he passed by had only one headline: NELSON! At 1.30 a.m., as he had slept soundly, a massive blast had exploded Nelson off his pillar and into smithereens. A small mountain of rubble had crashed down onto the street, windows of nearby buildings had shattered, and Dublin's streetscape was changed forever. After all the years of threats and arguments, Liam Sutcliffe had finally done it. Incredibly, no one was hurt. No one except Nelson, of course – he was done for.
The bomb hadn't destroyed the whole pillar, so now there was the problem of what

to do with a jagged, broken monument. It was decided to let the Irish army destroy it with a controlled explosion. On the day it was planned, people thronged the street to witness this historic moment. The army detonated their explosive – to a huge roar from the crowd – and promptly blew out any window that had been left standing after the original bombing. It became a joke told for many years around Dublin that the army had caused more damage than the original bomb!

As far as is known, just one bit of Nelson survived – his head. The massive granite head was taken from the street and put in storage, but about a week later there came an unexpected twist in the story. Nelson's head was stolen by a group of students from the National College of Art and Design (NCAD). They thought they could use it to make some money and pay off a debt. They were right. They hired the head of Nelson out for various purposes, including at parties, where Nelson was the special guest. They even managed to take it across to London and there hired it to an antiques dealer for the huge sum of £250 per month, and he put it in his window as a unique attraction. Eventually, though, the Gardaí tracked down the students, and the head, and Nelson's strange tour of duty was ended.

The spot where Nelson had stood was empty for a long time, but in 2003 the Spire was erected on the site. It is the tallest monument in Dublin at 121 m (397 ft) – it would have dwarfed Nelson in his day. So next time you're in Dublin and looking at the Spire glinting in the sun, try to 'see' the other layer of history beneath it – the long-resident and swiftly evicted Admiral Lord Nelson, a victim of history and circumstance. Who knows what he would have made of his own incredible Dublin story?

EXPLORE THE STORY

Lord Nelson's granite head is kept in the **Pearse Street Library** in Dublin. The bulletholes and pockmarks on it tell of the stories he witnessed on the streets below him.

ILLUSTRATED BY DONOUGH O'MALLEY

THE STORY OF MUHAMMAD ALI, 'IRISHMAN'

DO YOU KNOW WHO SAID THIS: 'IT ISN'T THE MOUNTAINS AHEAD TO CLIMB THAT WEAR YOU OUT; IT'S THE PEBBLE IN YOUR SHOE'? OR THIS: 'ONLY A MAN WHO KNOWS WHAT IT IS LIKE TO BE DEFEATED CAN REACH DOWN TO THE BOTTOM OF HIS SOUL AND COME UP WITH THE EXTRA OUNCE OF POWER IT TAKES TO WIN'? HOW ABOUT THIS: 'FLOAT LIKE A BUTTERFLY, STING LIKE A BEE. HIS HANDS CAN'T HIT WHAT HIS EYES CAN'T SEE. NOW YOU SEE ME, NOW YOU DON'T. GEORGE THINKS HE WILL, BUT I KNOW HE WON'T'? I'D SAY YOU GOT IT AT 'FLOAT LIKE A BUTTERFLY', DIDN'T YOU? YES, IT WAS THE ELECTRIFYING MUHAMMAD ALI – BOXER, WORD-WEAVER AND SUPERSTAR. BUT DID YOU KNOW HE WAS IRISH?

It was one of the biggest nights in the history of boxing – 8 March 1971, the 'Fight of the Century' in Madison Square Garden, New York. Around the world, 300 million people tuned in eagerly to watch. This was the moment to soar, to float, to sting, to win. The fight was brutal and intense, roared on by a live audience of thousands. Muhammad Ali lost.

In front of Madison Square Garden and the whole world, he was defeated by defending champion Joe Frazier. The heavyweight belt stayed in Frazier's hands.

What do you do after a defeat like that? How do you find your way back to believing you're a winner? How do you come back and set the record straight?

The following year, Ali set off on a boxing tour that would take him to six countries and thirteen fights. In July, he arrived in Ireland, ready to do battle against Al 'Blue' Lewis in Croke Park, home of hurling and Gaelic football. Now you must be thinking, why did a great sportsman like Ali come to Ireland and fight on a Gaelic Athletic Association (GAA) pitch? Who persuaded him to do such a thing? Ireland in the 1970s wasn't exactly a sports mecca and it didn't have much of a boxing tradition – this was a long time before world champion Katie Taylor would transform Irish boxing forever. So why would Ali agree to such an unusual and unexpected proposition?

The person who convinced the Ali team to include Ireland on his tour route was Michael 'Butty' Sugrue, and he was quite a character himself. Born in Kerry, he was once a strongman in the circus. He liked to boast that he could pull a double-decker bus by a rope clenched in his teeth. He was a man who didn't take no for an answer! When he first suggested that he could get Ali to fight in Ireland, everyone laughed at him – it seemed like a crazy notion. Ali wouldn't want to visit a tiny island in the Atlantic, would he? Butty must be away with the fairies! But Butty Sugrue was as determined as his strongman reputation suggested, and he persisted until word came through that, yes, the great Ali would add Dublin to his trail of fights.

The match was set for the night of 19 July 1972. On 11 July, Ali's plane touched down in Dublin Airport, allowing plenty of time for him to acquaint himself with Ireland and drum up business for the fight. Excitement was at fever pitch for this world-famous guest. When at last he descended the steps of the airplane and put his feet on Irish soil, one of his first pronouncements was that he had Irish roots – which astounded everyone!

It was true. No word of a lie. It turned out that an Irish emigrant called Abe Grady had left Ennis, County Clare, during the

1860s, to start a new life in America. He eventually ended up in Kentucky. He fell in love with an African-American woman who was an emancipated slave, and they married and had children. Abe Grady was Ali's great-grandfather, and Ali was returning now to the land Abe had left a hundred years before. Muhammad Ali had Irish blood running in his veins.

That bombshell announcement ignited a truly stupendous visit, with the whole country falling under Ali's mesmerizing spell, following him around the streets of Dublin, desperate to be near the great man, to hear him talk, to watch him fight. He met sportspeople, politicians, celebrities and ordinary people on the streets – and he was the same charming, mischievous man with all of them. He arrived an American but was quickly adopted as a prodigal Irish son.

In the other corner was Alvin 'Blue' Lewis, the boxer who would take on Ali in front of the crowd in Croke Park. His journey to Ireland was just as full of twists and turns. He was born and raised in Detroit, in a tough neighbourhood where he ran the streets with his fourteen brothers and sisters. His life took a wrong turn when he was sentenced to a minimum of twenty years in prison when he was only seventeen years old. In jail, he started boxing, and found that he was really good at it. He won the prison championship title five years in a row. After twelve years locked up, he was awarded early release after a prison riot, during which he saved a guard's life. When he got out, a local boxing promoter picked him up and put him to work. That was how he ended up in Dublin that summer. He saw cows for the first time and marvelled at how the sun didn't seem to set until midnight on those long evenings of high summer. Ireland was very, very different from the mean streets of Detroit.

The fight was the only thing on people's minds that week. When the day finally arrived, Croke Park was stuffed to the gills with a capacity crowd – but it's said that not many of those people had actually bought tickets. According to the legend that has grown around that fight, the majority of the crowd hopped over walls and turnstiles and pushed their way in to see this historic moment. They were all roaring one name: **'Ali! Ali! Ali!'**

The two fighters squared up for the twelve-round bout. They slugged it out, round after round. Finally, in the eleventh round, Lewis couldn't go on and the referee stopped the match. It was over. Ali had won. He was on his way back.

For Lewis, that was hard defeat to take. He had gone ten hard rounds with the champ, only to lose out late in the fight. But his prize money was some consolation – $35,000 and seven bottles of Guinness were tucked in his suitcase when he left. With that money, he was able to buy the first home the Lewis family had ever owned, a place for his mother to live out her days. So while he was sorry to lose, there was a silver lining for him.

Ali was still on his journey to be the best in the world. He stepped into the ring with Joe Frazier again in 1974, and this time he came out the winner. He had walked a hard road to get there, but now he could say he had defeated Frazier. It was 1–1.

The two rivals had one final match, known as the 'Thrilla in Manila'. That was in 1975, and it's remembered as one of the greatest fights ever staged. They beat each other senseless for fourteen long rounds, each refusing to give in to the other. Finally, Frazier's trainer stopped it, not letting his bloodied and battered fighter go out for round fifteen. And that was it – Ali had defeated Frazier again.

Ireland never forgot Muhammed Ali and the day Croke Park became a boxing ring. There are still stories about that night, and that week when Ali roamed around, delighting everyone who met him. He was a sportsman with the magnetism of a superstar. The idea of him being Irish as well was almost too good to be true.

He returned to Ireland in 2009 to visit County Clare, the birthplace of his great-grandfather, Abe Grady. He went to see where his bloodline had come from. By now, Ali was sixty-seven years old and living with Parkinson's disease, a much frailer man, robbed of the words he loved to spin like a spiderweb. But the love for him remained as strong as ever, and thousands came out to cheer his name and welcome him 'home'. He was made the first honorary freeman of the town of Ennis. The prodigal Irish son had returned and embraced his roots.

Muhammad Ali died in 2016. He had once been asked, when he was younger, how he would like to be remembered. In his inimitable way, Ali replied, 'As a man who never sold out his people. But if that's too much, then just a good boxer. I won't even mind if you don't mention how pretty I was.'

EXPLORE THE STORY

There is a monument to Muhammad Ali in **Ennis, County Clare**, commemorating his visit and his status as Honorary Freeman. Ali himself unveiled it during his visit and it stands as a testament to 'The Greatest' and his Irish roots.

ILLUSTRATED BY DONOUGH O'MALLEY

THE STORY OF THE PADDLE-BOARDERS, THE FISHERMEN AND TAYLOR SWIFT

HAVE YOU EVER DREAMED OF RESCUING SOMEONE AND BEING HAILED AS A HERO? IT MUST BE AN INCREDIBLE FEELING TO LEAP INTO ACTION WHEN SOMEONE NEEDS HELP AND TO KNOW THAT YOU HAVE SNATCHED THAT PERSON FROM THE VERY JAWS OF DEATH. IT MIGHT HAPPEN TO YOU DURING YOUR LIFE – IF YOU'RE IN THE RIGHT PLACE AT THE RIGHT TIME. BUT WHAT ARE THE CHANCES OF THAT HAPPENING TO A PERSON OVER AND OVER AGAIN?

August in Ireland is a good time for sea swimming – the water is a bit warmer than usual and the evenings are long and bright. On Furbo Beach in Galway, the sun was still warming the sand when two cousins, Sara Feeney and Ellen Glynn, prepared their inflatable paddleboards for an evening's paddling. There was only one catch – Ellen had forgotten her dry bag. This was a bag that she could put her mobile phone into without fear of it getting wet. She didn't have it, but she and Sara weren't worried – they were only going to go a bit out from the shore and then paddle parallel to the beach, like the swimmers were doing.

There's a saying in Ireland: if you don't like the weather, wait five minutes. It's always changing, never entirely predictable, which isn't a good thing when it comes to the water. On this evening, Sara and Ellen set out in lovely calm weather, enjoying the gentle breeze as they sculled past the swimmers and the rocks. But without warning, that gentle breeze grew into an insistent wind. When the girls turned for shore and tried to paddle back in, the wind was too strong. The reality of the situation was dawning on them – and it wasn't good.

As the wind picked up and the waves reached higher, the girls were pushed further away from the beach. They screamed for help, but the wind snatched their screams away. Ellen was only a teenager, just seventeen years old, but she stayed calm and forced herself to think straight. She had a buckle and she used it to tie the boards together. That was a really clever idea. They pushed down their fears. As Ellen said later, they didn't do 'out-loud worrying'. They only said positive things to each other – even as they drifted further and further out into wide Galway Bay.

The sun was dropping low, and the light started to fade. In Ellen's head, a song kept rattling around in circles. The words wouldn't leave her alone. 'I think I've seen this film before, and I didn't like the ending.' She began to sing it, just to push it out of her mind. At first, Sara was surprised by this sudden outburst, but then she started to sing along. They were singing Taylor Swift's song 'Exile', and it kept them calm as the open water took on the pitch black of the night sky above.

On the beach, Sara's mother had watched their progress, and then squinted to see them as they moved away. They were only wearing swimsuits and lifejackets – no wetsuits. How far had they gone? Worried, she raised the alarm and asked the coastguard to help. At 10 p.m., the search began.

Out on the choppy waters, the two boards floated side by side as the waves grew bigger. The girls paddled hard, trying to get back to shore. By now, it was too dark to see anything but distant lights. All around them, the sea was its own world, and they didn't belong there. They heard slaps and splashes, noises near and far, no way of knowing what was there because they couldn't see a thing. They were scared, but they weren't giving in to fear.

Around midnight, a beam of strong light lit up the waves. A helicopter! The girls waved and shouted, kneeling on their boards, but the helicopter couldn't hear them or see them. Around them, the sea was frightening but beautiful. They saw plankton drifting silently around them, they saw shooting stars whizzing through the darkness above. They saw things other people will never see.

On land, the girls' parents set out to search every nook and cranny from Clare to Galway, inching their way along the shore, never giving up. As they searched, rain started to fall, then there was a crack of thunder and a bright shard of lightning – a wild summer storm. No matter, they had to keep looking. Ellen's mother later said that as they searched, her mind was being bothered by a song that kept running on a loop, unending: 'I think I've seen this film before, and I didn't like the ending.'

The two cousins had no idea where they were or how far they had drifted, but they knew they couldn't see the lights on shore anymore. Around 3 a.m., the storm arrived. The swell rose up around them, buffeting their lashed-together boards, and over their heads the huge expanse of night sky was suddenly ripped by lightning, thunder echoing around them. The rain was so hard, it hurt their bare skin where it hit them. They watched as the helicopter turned and made for shore, unable to stay out in such threatening weather. And there they were, two little bodies, drifting on inflatable boards, with nothing to hold onto but each other.

When the sun finally began to rise, they were shaking with hypothermia, energy nearly spent. They looked around. They could see a lighthouse. They could see cliffs, and Sara guessed they were the Cliffs of Moher. Uh oh! That meant they were at the edge of Galway Bay, beyond Black Head, where the waters of the bay meet the waters of the wild Atlantic. If they kept drifting as they were, they would find themselves in the huge open expanse of the Atlantic Ocean – next stop, America. They were in real danger, and their bodies were suffering terribly from hypothermia. They spotted a float in the water, the kind that marks the location of a crab pot, and they made their way to it and realized it was anchored down, not floating. Hallelujah! They managed to tether the boards to the float, and finally, after about twelve hours of drifting away, they came to a stop.

Ellen lay down on her board and slept. After a time, Sara sat up and looked around, trying to figure out what to do next. In the distance, she saw a speck on the horizon. Could it be a boat? Was this a mirage, like an oasis in the desert? She watched and waited.

***

The search had been joined by hundreds of people, including fisherman Patrick Oliver and his teenage son, Morgan. The Olivers were a fishing family spanning generations, and they knew these waters. When they heard about the missing paddleboarders, Patrick and Morgan studied the local tide charts and calculated wind direction and speed. They turned their fast catamaran towards Black Head and sped off in search of the cousins. Out near Inis Oirr, Morgan saw something moving in the water. They made for it, and then realized it was two paddles being waved frantically in the air. They had them!

It was a miraculous rescue – miraculous that the girls had stayed calm and kept each other going, even through the storm, and miraculous that the Olivers had figured out their direction correctly and got there in time. The girls had travelled about 33 km (20.5 miles) in total. The Olivers pulled the two girls aboard and raced to Inis Oirr, from where the helicopter picked them up. The girls were safe, fifteen long hours after going missing, and the whole of Ireland was gobsmacked that this tragic tale turned out to have a happy ending.

Patrick and Morgan Oliver didn't want a fuss, but they were heroes, and everyone wanted to congratulate them. A few weeks later, they were out on the River Corrib when a call came in about a swimmer in trouble – and they rescued him. Talk about being in the right place at the right time – again! In October, a ceremony in Galway reunited the fishermen with the paddleboarders. They saw it as all in a day's work, but it was an extraordinary rescue.

Then, in November, tragedy struck. The Oliver family didn't have the rare luck of Ellen and Sara, and two Oliver fishermen died in fishing accidents. Life can be like a wave – it can carry you up, then dash you down. Fishermen respect the sea and obey its laws, but that doesn't always save them. But, incredibly, a few weeks after this terrible loss, Patrick and Morgan were out fishing at Salthill and spotted a swimmer beached on a rock, in distress. They went to that man and saved his life too. So many people owe the Olivers a huge debt of gratitude.

Sara and Ellen went back to their lives. To their astonishment, a letter arrived from Taylor Swift. She had heard about their awful adventure, and how her song had kept their spirits up, and she sent them a letter, along with a painting she had made. Music connects people in mysterious ways.

So, do you think the girls ever took to the water again? Well, one day, about a year later, Ellen decided it was time to paddleboard again. She went to the beach, prepared the board, checked the weather forecast, and decided she was going to do it.

All of sudden, the weather shifted, rain began to hammer down on the sand, and thunder and lightning broke out over the water. Ellen looked out at the waves … and went home.

Once a clever survivor, always a clever survivor!

EXPLORE THE STORY

A short film called **Sea of Souls** was made to commemorate the two Oliver fishermen who died, and all those who have lost their lives at sea. It captures a beautiful moment when 600 candles were floated out onto the Claddagh Basin in Galway while 'The Parting Glass' is sung. You can find it on YouTube.

ILLUSTRATED BY RÓISÍN HAHESSY

THE LAST PINGIN

BY LOLA-MAE McCORMACK, AGE 11

I took a penny from the full jar on my bedside table. It was a beautiful shiny copper, engraved with a mother hen walking with her five chicks and the letters 'pingin' in old Celtic font at the bottom. I had been saving my pennies for almost a year now, since my ninth birthday, when Mam told me that I was old enough to start collecting the eggs from the chicken coop. 'One penny for every unbroken egg,' she had said. I emptied the jar onto the floor and counted them. 169 pennies. I slipped the shiniest one into the hidden pocket sewn into my dress and replaced the lid on my jar.

Mam was waiting for me downstairs with her coins all counted into tiny plastic bags. Today we would bring our old coins to the bank and exchange them for the new decimal coins. There would be no more pennies, threepences, sixpences, crowns, shillings and farthings. From now on Ireland, like Britain, would use pounds and pennies. My mum was excited about the new money but I liked the old coins with their assortment of animals – the leaping salmon on the two shilling coin, the stomping bull on the one shilling, the proud horse on the half-crown, the hare ready to pounce off the threepence, the wolfhound on the sixpence and the pig and her piglets on the halfpence. My granny told me that these native animals were used on Ireland's very first coins in 1928 because of how important they were to our country. I wondered what the new decimal coins would look like. I was about

to find out – today was decimal day, the last day of the old money and the first day of the new.

It was a cold and wet Monday in February, so Mam and I took the bus to the bank. We paid the bus conductor with old money, which he added to the collection in his leather satchel and dispensed our tickets from the little machine around his neck. As we approached the final stop, I could see the queue for the bank through the steamy bus window.

The long queue that snaked out the door of the bank moved painstakingly slow and Mam's excitement started to wane as she let out a long, tired sigh. A small breeze started up, and my pale blue dress swirled around my legs, teasing my ankles. I could feel the weight of my hidden penny tapping against my leg in the breeze and I knew it was safe.

I'd never been to the bank before – it seemed like a very important place that only adults went to. But today it was crowded with confused adults and children of all ages, all waiting to change their old Irish money. When it was finally my turn, I looked at the pennies in my jar one last time and thought of all the eggs I'd gathered to earn them. I slid the jar onto the metal tray and watched sadly as the well-dressed bank teller counted out my coins, exchanging the old for the new. I waited eagerly for my new coins and imagined the jar spilling over with shiny new money. The teller slowly counted out my new coins. 168 old pennies were worth just 70p! Instead of 168 coins, I now had only seven. It didn't seem fair! I looked at Mam waiting for her to say that it must be wrong but she just moved forward to exchange her own money. Confused and disappointed, I put the coins in my purse and took back the empty jar. As I waited for Mam I saw other children and older people looking equally disheartened and confused. Some were annoyed and arguing with the bank tellers that they had counted the new money incorrectly. At

school they told us that it would be easier to work in the tens and hundreds of the decimal system but right now it just seemed confusing.

We walked back to the bus stop in silence. Mam excitedly paid with our new coins but the bus conductor refused, explaining angrily that he wasn't taking any new coins today as they wouldn't fit in his machine. With aching feet and lighter pockets, we walked home. Mam and I spread the new coins on the kitchen table – I had a 50p, 10p, 5p, 2p, 1p and two half pennies. They all had a harp on one side, and different Celtic designs or animals on the other. I flipped them over one by one looking for my hen, the horse, the bull, the hare… The salmon and the bull were still there, but my hen with her chicks were not there on the new coins, they were gone. In place of my chicks, the new penny had a swirling, beautiful ornamental bird.

That night, as I changed into my pyjamas, I looked at the empty jar on my bedside table. Tomorrow morning I would collect eggs with the promise of adding my first new copper halfpenny, which also featured an intricate engraving of an ornamental bird on one side and an Irish harp on the other. I liked it, but I missed my hen and her five chicks. I took my last, special pingin from my secret pocket and placed it carefully under my pillow. Pingin, you will always be my lucky penny.

....

ILLUSTRATED BY RÓISÍN HAHESSY

ACKNOWLEDGEMENTS

A huge and heartfelt thank you to
Leah James, Faith O'Grady, Philip Parker,
Matthew Grundy Haigh, Aimee Stewart,
Donough O'Malley, Erin Brown, Eva Byrne,
Jennifer Davison, Linda Fahrlin,
Lydia Hughes, Róisín Hahessy
and Úna Woods.

Love and gratitude to
Donagh, Erris, Meeda and
Conne McCarthy.

ABOUT THE AUTHOR

RACHEL PIERCE lives in Drogheda, on the east coast
of Ireland. Rachel loves to explore Ireland and its
history on adventures with her three children.

Rachel is also the author of
Ireland: The People, The Places, The Stories.

ABOUT THE ILLUSTRATORS

DONOUGH O'MALLEY

Donough O' Malley is an award-winning illustrator from County Monaghan in the north east of Ireland. As well as illustrating children's books, he also creates illustrations for just about everything else, from magazines to toy packaging, for people all over the world.

ERIN BROWN

Erin is a Northern Irish illustrator who lives and works on the beautiful island of Jersey. She combines her love for hand-drawn lines and traditional techniques with the flexibility and freedom of adding colour digitally. Her love of stories comes from her grandad who lived by the sea and was always ready with a tale or two.

EVA BYRNE

Eva lives on the West Coast of Ireland, working as a freelance illustrator for publishers, advertising agencies, and magazines for over 20 years but she is a children's book Illustrator at heart. Her first children's book, written by Savannah Gurthrie and Alison Oppenheimer, *Princesses Wear Pants*, became a *New York Times* Bestseller.

JENNIFER DAVISON

Jennifer is an illustrator from Northern Ireland. She works at home, in her little studio packed full of children's books and toys. She loves the playfulness of producing work for children. It takes her back to being a child herself, spending hours creating imaginary worlds and characters.

LINDA FARHLIN

Linda is an illustrator based on the North West coast of Ireland. Her illustrative style is influenced by her Swedish heritage and from her studio, she works as a visual artist and illustrates children's books, book covers and commercial illustrations.

LYDIA HUGHES

Lydia is an illustrator and designer based in Westport, County. Mayo. She graduated with a BA in Visual Communication from Herefordshire College of Arts and practised as a visual designer in the UK, Canada and Ireland before going on to complete an MA in Illustration with the University of Hertfordshire.

RÓISÍN HAHESSY

Róisín was born and raised in Ireland, moved to Brazil in 2015 and has recently relocated to Portugal. Changing cultures, climate and so much more has really inspired Róisín and her art over the last few years. When she isn't drawing, she loves nothing more than snuggling up in a cosy corner with a good book or a film.

ÚNA WOODS

Úna Woods is an illustrator and writer from Ireland. She loves to create magical illustrations for young children using quirky and cute characters and animals. She works digitally combining simple shapes, patterns and bright colours.

Photo by Ruth Medjber Photography

152

INDEX

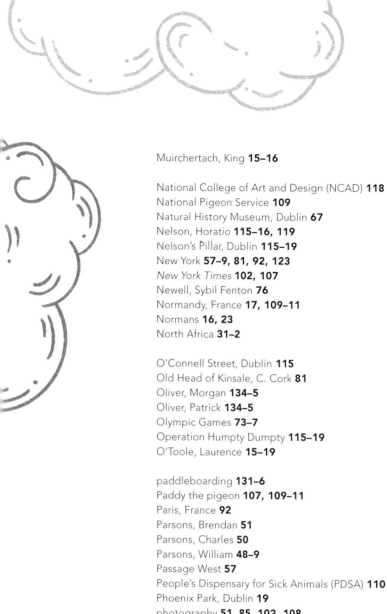